HOUSEPLANTS AND HARDCOVERS

DAPHNE JAMES HUFF

For internet friends, new and old.

ONE

November

APRIL

Pete the prayer plant was dying.

If Juliet was being honest with herself, he had been dying for a while. Then she'd gone into one of her super-concentrated work sprints and did nothing but sleep and copyedit for four days. Now most of her plants looked less than well-loved, sagging sadly over the edge of their pots between teetering stacks of books, but poor Pete had suffered the worst.

Juliet leaned in, examining his leaves in the sunlight streaming through her home office's windows. Unlike Pete, Juliet had gotten some nourishment this week, but only because her mom had sent food over. Almost twenty years since she left home, she still regularly needed to be watered and fed by someone else.

A buzzing from her desk drew her attention away from her plants. Her phone was ringing. She didn't have to look to know it was her mom. No one else called her.

"Did you get the salad?"

"Hello to you too." Juliet tucked the blanket she was wearing over her shoulders even tighter so it draped behind her like a cape. "Yes, I got it."

"Did you eat it?"

"Yes." Not immediately, but within twelve hours. That counted as the same meal, didn't it?

Her mother sighed, as if she'd guessed at Juliet's unspoken words. "It shouldn't be this hard to keep my thirty-seven-year-old daughter alive." The sounds of nature chirped through the phone, along with the babble of a toddler. "Your sister doesn't need this kind of attention. Her small children do."

"So stop sending the salads. I can take care of myself."

"You can't even keep those plants alive."

Juliet had no argument there. Here she was, staring at five shriveled brown leaves on a prayer plant that looked like it was praying to be put out of its misery.

"The plants were your idea. You should be the one to take care of them." The bitterness in her words got another sigh from her mother. Like she needed another reminder about how incompetent she was at managing her own life.

"I water them every time I come over. Or rather, whenever you let me come over."

The itch to get back to her computer and escape this conversation was a thousand writhing ants crawling up her arms. In front of a page, with stylistic errors and typos to be corrected, Juliet was in total control. When online reputations and major financial deals could be ruined forever from a misplaced comma, nothing was more important than the right editor. Her clients' only concern was that she got their manuscripts polished to perfection in record time. They didn't care if she could keep a plant alive.

Juliet tugged gently at the brownest of Pete's leaves, and it slipped off the stem as if attached by only the flimsiest of threads. The prayer plant needed her more than her clients right now, it seemed.

Thank goodness her mother hadn't bought her a cat.

"You can come over tonight, if you want," Juliet said, turning away from Pete to look at the calendar above her desk. "I just finished a deadline, so I don't have much work for the next few days."

"It'll have to wait, sweetie, Allison needs me to watch the boys overnight."

The sting of rejection shouldn't be as sharp after all these years, but there it was. Her mother complained Juliet never wanted her to come over, but then was too busy when she did invite her. Juliet took a deep breath and the pain in her chest eased a bit, though not completely.

"Well, whenever you have time. I'm always here," she said.

"That's what worries me the most. You should get out of the house more."

"Mom, I work at home."

"Exactly. You live your whole life inside." There was a loud squawk from her mother's end of the phone—one of the kids must have seen a dog or something. "Allison's husband just finished his third Ironman this weekend. He almost qualified for the world championships."

"I know. I saw the pictures." Juliet plopped down in her office chair, curled her legs to her chest, and pulled the blanket over herself.

"You could have seen it in person."

"I had a deadline." Also, it had been a three-hour drive to the mountain town to Tony's race. There was no way she would have been able to do that, even if she still had a car.

"I would have driven you." Again, it was as if her mom had guessed the words she'd held back.

Now if only she could pick up on Juliet's desire to get off the phone and back to her plant disaster.

"Next time. I have to go. I'll call you in a few days."

After saying their goodbyes, Juliet hung up and stood up, the blanket dropping to the floor. Rather than deal with the emotions a five-minute phone call had dredged up, she switched to her camera to take a picture of the dying plant. Then, it was just another swipe of her thumb and a few taps of her fingers to pull open the social media app where normally she'd post about the open space in her editing calendar. Instead, she went into the private-messaging section to send the photo to the one person who could help her right now.

Plantsguy95.

There was already a message waiting for her, a laughing emoji in response to a meme she'd sent him a few days ago. From that initial message a few months ago—when her mother had dropped off five plants and they'd all been drooping within a week—an easy online friendship had blossomed.

Blossomed. She almost groaned out loud at the plant pun. That was undoubtedly his influence. He was funny with words in a way she could never achieve without hours of contemplation first.

The little green dot next to his profile picture—a leafy green *Ficus*—let Juliet know he was online. A reply came almost immediately to her picture of a dying Pete.

PLANTSGUY95

What happened?

JCEDITS

I got busy with work.

PLANTSGUY95

Isn't this one in the bathroom like I suggested, for the humidity?

Did you not go to the bathroom for a week?

JCEDITS

I plead the fifth.

PLANTSGUY95

JC, you gotta be nicer to your body. Forget about the plants.

Juliet snorted. Though it went against all sorts of best practices for using social media to grow your business, she didn't share her name unless someone was a client. Plantsguy95 only knew her as JCEdits, her username, which he turned into JC.

JCEDITS

I'm screenshotting that and showing all your 15 million followers you said that.

PLANTSGUY95

15 million?

Wow, it must have gone up by 14.99 million since yesterday.

JCEDITS

You mean you don't check your followers?

You have like, five times as many as me, and people share your stuff all the time.

PLANTSGUY95

This isn't my full-time gig.

It's not even a gig. I don't get paid for this.

I just want people to learn about plants.

For someone with close to twenty thousand followers, Plantsguy95 had a very laid-back approach to his account that Juliet couldn't understand. Not for the first time, she wondered what his real job was . . . and his name. Neither of them posted pictures of themselves, so she didn't even know what he looked like. All his photos were plants, sometimes with hands she assumed were his, sometimes his shadow. Her account was entirely copyediting tips and memes, her profile photo a stylized red pen.

She knew he was a *he* from the pronouns in his bio, but beyond that, it was frustratingly bare bones, even more anonymous than Juliet's. At least hers told the world what she did and how to contact her. All his said was "I'm a guy who likes plants. I answer your #solvemyplantproblem questions every Wednesday." No location, no link to a website or even a fundraising campaign.

Juliet never took social media clients, since she charged by word, and it was not the most efficient use of her time. This was a dire situation, however, and exceptions had to be made. Within minutes, he sent a comprehensive list of everything Juliet needed to do, almost hour by hour, to make sure Pete survived. The tension that had built up over the last four days dropped off Juliet's shoulders. It was reassuring to see something so organized. Now that she felt like the plant part of her life was under control, she could get back to work.

Lucas was in the middle of his shift at the hardware store when he got an update from JC about the prayer plant she'd ignored into drought. It was still drooping a week after he'd told her how to save it, but "since it's technically still alive," she said he could send her the posts he wanted her to write.

His lips curved up into a smile wider than the hacksaws he was pricing as he tapped out a reply.

PLANTSGUY95

Are you sure your prayer plant doesn't have a death wish?

JCEDITS

The thought has crossed my mind. I thought I was a good roommate.

No complaints from the others, though.

PLANTSGUY95

How many others do you have?

JCEDITS

Roommates or plants?

PLANTSGUY95

I already know how many plants you have, since I've had to keep them all from dying from lack of attention.

JCEDITS

And how many is that?

PLANTSGUY95

10.

JCEDITS

Ha! I have 12 plants.

I kept the Aloe plants alive all by myself.

PLANTSGUY95

I'm positively bursting with pride.

JCEDITS

Don't get too proud, you haven't saved the prayer plant yet.

She'd avoided the roommate question, and while it might

not have been intentional, it did remind him that she wasn't that kind of online friend. Personal details shared were minimal. They never talked much about family or friends. She only mentioned her work when it got in the way of her plant care.

Leaning against a shelf full of boxes of nails, Lucas ran a hand through his hair and stared down at his phone, like he could hypnotize it into giving him the information he wanted.

The internet was an amazing thing. You could look up the answers to literally any question, as Lucas liked to remind his family when they blew up his phone with their bonkers requests at three in the morning. Though at least his grandmother waited until the sun was up.

The internet, however, could not solve the question he'd been wondering about for months, despite the embarrassing amount of hours he'd spent sleuthing.

Who was JCEdits?

All he knew for sure was that she was an editor. A few years ago, he would have traded all his plant advice until the end of time to get professionally written and edited posts. What had started as a failed side hustle had turned into an unexpected way to connect with other plant nerds outside of his small town. It wasn't to make money or get famous, at least not anymore. Not since his ex—and his reason for starting the account—was no longer in the picture. Now, he just wanted to talk to people about plants and help them learn more about them.

A few short months ago, JC had been completely clueless. Even worse than his cousin Marigold—Mari—who'd managed to kill a cactus in two days by mixing up the saltwater she'd put in a bottle for her facial routine with . . . well, it didn't really matter since he'd told her at least five times succulents don't need daily watering.

JC was a quick learner though. Since Lucas loved nothing more than people who asked him questions about the things he loved most, they'd been chatting a few times a week since her first timid message asking for help with her brand-new plant babies.

It was nice, in a way, to have something that was light and low pressure. The opposite of his life with a huge family that lived and breathed drama like they were trying out to be the next reality TV sensation.

And yet . . . he really wanted to know if JC lived with anyone.

Instead of asking again, he looked up from his phone to make sure he was still alone in the aisle, and focused his response to her on the plants, like he was expected to.

PLANTSGUY95

Why don't you try your local horticultural society?

JCEDITS

I'm sorry, my local what now?

This isn't the 1800s and I am not a romance heroine with nothing to do until an appropriate suitor comes to call.

PLANTSGUY95

Fine, garden club, if you prefer.

JCEDITS

Also not a 1950s housewife waiting for her husband to come home to beat him over the head with a leg of lamb.

He chuckled, and the noise caught his boss's attention. Normally, Henry didn't care about phone use during work. But whenever Henry's dad, who owned the store, was around, the rules suddenly became stricter. So Lucas stashed his phone in his back pocket and got back to pricing boxes of nails under

Henry's watchful eye. It was an agonizing three hours before Lucas could reply to JC's message.

His shift finally over, Lucas practically threw his apron at Henry and ran out of the hardware store, passing a row of smaller shops on his way to the back parking lot that employees used. The evening was warm for early spring, and he inhaled a lungful of crisp air as he leaned against the side of his truck and thought about what to tell JC. It was a fine line to walk between revealing too much about himself and coming off as insincere.

The choice to never show his face in the account kept him anonymous. Plants were his main focus on the account, not making it his identity, his business, his life. That hadn't gone very well the first time he'd tried it, as the harsh criticisms of his ex had so generously pointed out.

Besides, Greenhaven was on the smaller side. Five square miles with an adorable store-lined, cobblestone main street that would make Norman Rockwell proud, and a gossip mill that put Hollywood tabloids to shame. Lucas knew word would get around if he put his face out there, then *everyone* would have something to say about it. It was enough trouble as it was to have his younger cousins weigh in on his very outdated use of hashtags.

Now, however, he wished he could tell JC about the garden club in Greenhaven that he'd belonged to since he was old enough to hold a spade.

PLANTSGUY95

Google the name of your city + horticultural society or garden club, to see what comes up.

Most cities of a certain size have one, even if it's just a few people who get together to trade seeds.

JCEDITS

"Trade seeds" huh?

Is that what the kids these days are calling it?

He laughed out loud at that one, then looked around to make sure no one had seen him. Laughing to himself in a deserted parking lot behind Main Street wasn't exactly his best look. Not to mention if Henry spotted him, he'd probably assume Lucas had nowhere to be tonight and ask him to work a few more hours.

Before he could forget, he drafted a post on garden clubs to share with his followers, giving a bit of the history and importance that they served in communities. It took an enormous amount of restraint to not add anything specific to his town, since he honestly thought they were one of the best in his area. The work they did in Greenhaven was incredible, and not just because his family had done so much of it.

Now dangerously close to having Henry come out and ask him to help close the store, Lucas got into his truck—even years after he passed, it was still hard to not think of it as his grandfather's old truck—to drive to his grandmother's house. On his way, he passed town hall, where the rows of planters were fresh and colorful thanks to the club. Two people chatted away on the nearby bench as the sky turned darker, oblivious to the months of fundraising the garden club had done to get it installed.

Typical. He sighed as he turned onto a side street. *No one appreciates a really good garden.*

There was a family crossing the street to the library, which was lit up inside for some evening event, and Lucas stopped the truck to let them pass. A few buildings down, his cousin Sage's car was parked in front of the garden club, and a light was on.

Their grandmother was still the elected president of the Greenhaven Garden Club, but she'd gotten sick over the winter.

Then her best friend had died, and Granny just didn't seem to like being out and about as much. They'd scheduled an election for the next meeting to select an acting president, but for now, the other members rotated duties.

Except Sage wasn't technically a member. She was family, and the Geis family helped each other no matter what. So without a second's hesitation, Lucas pulled into the driveway behind her car, whatever plans he'd had for the evening put on hold in favor of something much more important.

TWO

The early spring night was cool, and Juliet was enjoying the short walk from her apartment to the library for an emergency meeting of the Friends of the Greenhaven Library.

When she'd first moved into town, joining was the only activity she could think of to get her mom off her back about getting outside and contributing to her new community. The early access to their used book sales had been the main draw, but it didn't hurt that most of the members were retired and just as introverted as Juliet. After all, there was a reason she worked for herself from home and all of her closest friends were online.

The last-minute meeting was quite mysterious since Denise Thomas, the president of the Friends, had been vague in her email. At least it was close to Juliet's house, another reason she'd chosen this organization to invest her time in. On the way there, she passed in front of the old Victorian mansion that was listed online as the address for the town's garden club.

She'd looked up the club just as Plantsguy95 had suggested. Their meetings were only once a month, and their last one had been a few days ago. She should update him and ask if he had any other tips on how Pete could survive another few weeks until someone could take a look in person.

It was a gorgeous house, with delicate plant carvings around the huge windows and scrolled ivy woodwork on the wraparound porch. There was a banner stretched across the front of the house, advertising that their upcoming plant sale was happening that weekend. Warm relief rushed through Juliet's chest. Pete wouldn't have to wait three weeks after all.

Arriving at the door to the library, she took out her phone. Her finger hovered over the message box, uncertain, and she worried her bottom lip with her teeth as she reread her last exchange with Plantsguy95 from a few days ago. Her joke about trading seeds seemed embarrassingly suggestive now. She didn't think of him in that way, at least, not in any serious way. How could she, when she didn't even know his name?

It did always give her a boost to make him laugh, or at least, to entertain him enough to get an amused emoji. Which he hadn't sent in response this time. It didn't matter, though, because all she was looking for right now was friendship. That it was all her bruised and battered heart could handle at the moment.

Instead, she swiped over to a new message from Charlotte—username EditsALottie—one of the first friends she'd made online when she'd launched her business over ten years ago. They'd even met in person from time to time at conferences, where the extremely outgoing Charlotte always managed to introduce Juliet to about eight hundred people in twelve minutes. Juliet was tired just thinking about it.

EDITSALOTTIE

Did you see the BOCs have opened up for submissions?

Juliet checked the clock. She had another ten minutes before the meeting started. Plenty of time to answer Charlotte.

JCEDITS

Already? Are you entering this year?

EDITSALOTTIE

I dunno, I'm deep in a technical handbook update, not sure I'll have the time to put something together.

You should totally submit though.

JCEDITS

Nothing recent seems like a good fit. The winners are always something artsy, like an exhibit catalog or magazine.

Most of my work this year was academic journals.

What about that novel you did? It hit a bestseller list, didn't it?

EDITSALOTTIE

Ugh, I just saw they changed the rules this year.

No work that was done for publishing houses.

JCEDITS

That's the only non-academic work I've done.

So unless something comes up in the next day or two, looks like it won't happen for me this year.

EDITSALOTTIE

You'll still come to the conference though, won't you?

Two fun-filled days of me. I mean, "informational sessions."

I'll be there as long as our alumni thing isn't the same weekend. It's even in your state this year.

JCEDITS

I don't know yet . . . it's on the other side of the state.

Not a huge fan of driving.

It sounded like a weak excuse when she reread it, but it was as close to the truth as Juliet felt like getting with Charlotte. Even if she wanted to see her friend, it wasn't worth the stress of getting there, and then a full two days of smiling and pretending she was happy to be in the middle of all that chaos.

It could be worth it, if she was up for a BOC, however. The Best of Copyediting awards were, in the grand scheme of things, not that big a deal. Juliet had plenty of clients without it, and testimonials and referrals counted for way more than a little badge on her website.

The real reason she wanted to win was so petty that Juliet hated to admit it, even to herself: it would be something her mother could understand and appreciate. Not quite as brag-worthy as an Ironman medal or a fancy title and corner office like her sister had, but a prize was a prize.

Until that unlikely scenario, however, Juliet could keep her mom happy with things like volunteering for local community organizations. Sighing, she walked into the library, gave a smile to Patrice behind the desk, and on a whim, an uncharacteristic wave.

The wave must have been too much, she realized with a cringe. The white-haired man narrowed his eyes at her.

"Hello, Patrice." She slowed her steps and swallowed hard, taking a deep breath to calm her jangled nerves before opening her mouth to speak. "Where's the emergency Friends meeting tonight?"

Eyes still narrowed, he waved a wrinkled and sun-spotted pale hand in the direction of the stairs. "New members need to pay dues before attending their first meeting."

He's almost ninety, Juliet reminded herself, and closed her eyes to hold back the tears. *He doesn't recognize a lot of people.*

Before she found the words to convince him that she did indeed belong here, Juliet heard her voice from upstairs.

"Ah, Juliet, wonderful." A pair of big, brown eyes crinkled in a smiling, warm-bronze face as the president of the Friends of the Library peered over the banister. Denise was a middle-aged woman who Juliet had never seen in a bad mood in the year she'd known her. "You're the last one. Hurry on up before Miss Elsie eats all the chocolate chip and there's only oatmeal raisin left."

Juliet widened her eyes dramatically. "Who brought oatmeal raisin cookies?"

"My wife," Patrice said behind her.

While Denise just shook her head and chuckled, Juliet's stomach sank. This was why she never attempted spontaneous humor. Hopefully Patrice would have forgotten who she was again by the next time she came in.

The small meeting room upstairs was full of boxes of books and chattering Friends, the air buzzing with the mystery of why Denise had called a meeting on such short notice. A few people wondered if this was an appeal to use someone's garage or base-ment. The small storage room the Friends had downstairs was overflowing. Juliet smiled politely at all of them before shoving a cookie into her mouth. She'd already insulted one person tonight, and she'd rather not make it another twenty.

Not that anyone approached her to talk. In the six months since she'd joined, only Denise had talked to her for more than a brief hello. Juliet's fingers itched to take out her phone and share her awkwardness with someone, anyone, online where she wouldn't have to see their judgment on their face, just read their encouraging words.

Denise clapped her hands twice and the conversations fizzled out, along with Juliet's last chance to sneak out quietly with a few cookies. She leaned against a wall between two stacks of boxes and turned her eyes to Denise.

"Thank you all for coming on such short notice. I'll follow up with an email with more details, but this was such exciting news. I wanted to see all of your faces when you heard it."

"You can see us on a video call too," someone grumbled behind Juliet.

Agreed.

"We've just received a huge donation, the largest in the Friend's history." Denise's eyes sparkled with excitement at the murmur of interest that rippled through the room. Even Juliet's heart beat a little faster. "My grandfather, George Thomas, started the Friends by selling his own private book collection over sixty years ago, but this surpasses even that.

"The Periwinkle Mansion on Main Street has been left to the Friends in the last will and testament of Maude Periwinkle, who passed at the end of last year."

It was obvious she was about to burst out of her skin with excitement, but Denise's clear and measured tone and pace remained appropriate for the somber source of this good fortune.

"Isn't that where the garden club meets?" The man behind Juliet asked, his voice a grumpy rasp even when at full volume. "They've been there for decades. Maude let them use it."

Juliet hadn't realized the huge yellow house she'd passed earlier had a name. The Periwinkle Mansion sounded so fancy and official, appropriate for her idealized images of a garden club.

Denise blinked once, her smile frozen. "It seems Ms. Periwinkle wants us to use it now. The will's been through probate and her intentions were very clear. She gave it to the Friends of the Library to use 'in the service of the Greenhaven community' were her exact words. There's no mention of the garden club at all with regards to the house."

The rest of the room let out approving murmurs, Denise's excitement finally catching. Only the grumbler seemed unhappy. Juliet turned her head, feigning a look at the books piled next to her to avoid suspicion, and took a peek at him. His dark hair was laced with silver, and by the stern set of his eyebrows and rigidity of his crossed arms, was the only person in the room not totally thrilled about this news.

Well, technically Juliet wasn't thrilled, but she wasn't upset either. She was pleasantly neutral, her preferred state. The garden club would use another building, the Friends would have more space for their used book donations, and Juliet's life would go on in much the same way it had before.

"The bequest includes all contents of the house not specifically left to others, so it needs to be cleared out before we can start using it."

Now the reason for the in-person meeting was clear. It was much easier to avoid a call to volunteer by email than to do it with Denise's kind eyes staring at you.

Juliet quietly bit into another cookie and looked down at the ground.

"Can I have a few volunteers to go in a few hours next week to sort through it all?"

She couldn't see it behind her, but the grumbler's hand must have gone up. Denise arched an eyebrow.

"Stephen? You want to head up this initiative?"

"Absolutely."

There was a pause, while Denise waited for more details on why he was so enthusiastic about what sounded like hard, monotonous work. To be fair, Juliet knew others thought that about her work as a copy editor. Maybe Stephen liked sorting through papers and books, putting everything in order, just like Juliet enjoyed the feeling of smoothing out someone else's words to perfection.

When there was nothing further from him as an explanation, Denise cleared her throat.

"Great, we'll find some time this week to get you a set of keys." She turned to the rest of the group. "Now, Ms. Periwinkle also left a huge donation of used books, so I was thinking we should move up our next book sale to this weekend. Can those who volunteered for next month make the new date work?"

Juliet didn't even have to think about it. Every weekend was the same for her—devoid of plans—and volunteers got first pick of the books before the sale started. She raised her hand, along with a dozen others. Denise smiled widely at them all, then launched into the logistics of moving the date. The meeting ended about ten minutes later.

When Juliet left, Stephen and Denise were in what looked like a weighty discussion, their expressions bursting with irritation. The familiar tug of being left out warred with Juliet's desire for peace. Whatever petty disagreement they had was none of her concern, she reminded herself. The less drama in her life, the better.

THREE

"Lucas, darling, we've lost the house."

Hot panic shot into Lucas's veins at his grandmother's words and the label maker he was holding slipped from his hand. It clattered onto the linoleum and drew Henry's glare from across the store where he was standing with his dad.

"Geis, that better not be broken."

Lucas waved Henry's concern away and bent to pick it up, his other hand still gripping the phone close to his ear.

"And no phone calls when on the floor."

"It's my grandmother," he shouted back.

Henry's face softened and he nodded at Lucas.

Everyone liked Granny Geis. The epitome of Sweet Old Lady, she regularly brought baked goods to wherever Lucas was working. Since Lucas had worked in just about every business in Greenhaven, Granny was basically the town's grandmother now. She gave so much to others, without ever asking for anything in return. She remembered every name, every detail people decided to share with her.

Not to mention she'd probably changed a few of Henry's

diapers when he was a baby, which Lucas would remind him of, if needed, to bring him down a peg or two.

"Your house is paid off, Granny. What are you talking about?" Lucas made his way to the back room, taking the slightly bent label maker with him. Laying it on the small round table in the staff-only area, he opted to stand rather than sit in one of the squeaky plastic chairs. This felt like a pacing kind of conversation.

"Not my house," Granny said as Lucas passed in front of the staff bulletin board plastered with legal notices and shift schedules. "The garden club's. Maude Periwinkle left it to the Friends of the Library in her will."

"I thought the garden club owned it." Lucas had reached the door and turned around to repeat his circuit in the opposite direction. "The meetings have always been there. There's a picture of you, Granny, at the house when you joined in, what? 1960?"

"We've been using it for as long as the club's existed, but only because Maude was the first president."

"Then why would she leave it to the Friends? It makes no sense." Lucas could feel his blood heat. He'd just been there a few days ago with Sage, and there'd been no indication that anything was going to happen. "You should challenge the will."

"There's no reason to." She didn't even sound upset, just tired. The heat in Lucas's veins ticked up a notch. This was not the kind of stress Granny needed right now, not after what she'd been through this winter. Losing Maude had been hard enough, and now they were losing her house.

"There were never any promises from Maude, no formal agreement. We just met at her house because we always had. When she went into the long-term facility last year, she told me over the phone we could keep using it, but nothing about—"

Her voice caught. "About what she wanted to happen to it after."

Lucas's heart was breaking in two for her. "The Friends can't just take a house that means so much to you, to the club."

"The Friends aren't taking anything. It was a gift from Maude."

"She was your best friend. This doesn't make any sense."

"It's because I was her best friend that I need to honor her last wishes."

Having already abandoned his pacing, Lucas flopped into a squeaky chair and ran a hand through his hair.

"Did you just find out today?"

There was a pause on the other end. Lucas took the phone away from his ear to make sure it was still connected. "Granny?"

She sighed. "I've known for a while now. I was just waiting for the right time to tell you. Denise told the Friends last night, so everyone in town will know by the end of today one way or another."

Ah yes, the Greenhaven gossip train. Chief engineers: the Geis Gals, otherwise known as Lucas's cousins.

"Why didn't you tell me? Or the club?"

"I didn't want anyone to get upset, especially you. I know how . . . spirited you can get about things. No sense bothering the Friends about it, it's not their fault."

A snort escaped Lucas's mouth. "No, they're just getting the best piece of real estate in town for free, for no good reason."

"Maude must have had her reasons."

"Or she had no reason." An idea sparked for Lucas. "Are you sure she was of sound mind when she made the will?"

"Since it was written ten years ago, yes."

"And she never mentioned anything to you? That seems suspicious."

Granny sighed again, the long, slow one that meant Lucas

was severely trying her patience. Guilt rippled through him. Now *he* was the kind of stress she didn't need right now.

"I'm sorry, Granny." He grabbed the label maker in one hand and squeezed the handle, accidentally pricing the table at $5.99. Definitely way too high for the dented and worn Formica. "It's just a big shock."

"Well, please deal with your shock in a healthy way that does not involve pitchforks and torches. Remember what happened when you started that petition to save Harvey's Hamburgers."

"A few rats in the back parking lot is not a reason to deprive the town of a culinary institution."

Cutting off what could have turned into one of Lucas's hours-long rants, Granny wisely switched topics.

"You should get back to work. I'll see you for dinner? Mari is bringing her new boyfriend."

Only because Granny wasn't there to scold him, he rolled his eyes. "Can't wait."

They said goodbye and hung up.

Though he knew he should get back out on the floor, he immediately switched into battle mode, shooting off a few texts to his cousins, the beginnings of a plan already forming.

His grandmother knew him well—he was definitely going to do something about this, *with* pitchforks and torches if necessary. How could he not? Granny loved that house. The club had been using it for decades. There was no way Maude had suddenly changed her mind about one of the most important pieces of her estate without a reason.

Not to mention, the Friends of the Library seemed like a totally random choice. Greenhaven wasn't that big of a town, so being on multiple boards and helping with at least a few different organizations was common. But Maude had always been just the garden club, nothing else. At least, as far as Lucas knew.

The one person he wouldn't ask more about it was Granny. Though it hadn't been unexpected, Maude's death had hit her hard. Her voice had been steady on the phone just now, but Lucas knew his grandmother just as well as she knew him. Granny was hurting deep inside and always would.

Feeling slightly calmer after a few of his cousins responded with the appropriate amount of outrage, he swiped over to his social media. The account had really grown a lot in the last year, but there was no way for him to use it in this situation, not without giving up his anonymity. He scrolled through the long list of messages and stopped on one from JCEdits. It was from a few days ago, but he'd missed it somehow.

JCEDITS

I found a local garden club. I think I'll stop by their plant sale with Pete.

Thanks for the tip.

It was a simple message, accompanied by a ridiculous GIF, but it lifted his spirits in an unexpected way. Until he reread and his eyes caught on "Pete."

Maybe a cousin. Lucas had more than enough of those. Or a brother. But this could also be her subtle way of telling him she had a boyfriend, or a husband. It shouldn't have bothered Lucas to discover that she wasn't single. He'd never met her, didn't know what she looked like, and for all he knew, she might live on the other side of the country. There was no chance of them ever meeting. He didn't even know her name. It shouldn't matter.

The green dot let him know she was online, so rather than add fuel to his foul mood, he asked the question before he could chicken out.

PLANTSGUY95

Anytime. I hope you and Pete pick up some nice plants at the sale.

JCEDITS

Yes, he needs a new friend.

I had to cut off all his brown leaves except for 2.

Relief washed over Lucas, warm and fresh like summer rain.

PLANTSGUY95

Pete the Prayer Plant?

JCEDITS

I know it's silly to name my plants.

But they're alive. It seems weird to call them "it," you know?

PLANTSGUY95

Don't worry, I name my plants too. All real plant parents do.

JCEDITS

You're just saying that to be nice.

PLANTSGUY95

No, really. Right now there's Angela, Pamela, Sandra, and Rita.

JCEDITS

Pretty sure those are just "Mambo Number Five" lyrics.

PLANTSGUY95

Hey, I didn't say I give them unique or creative names.

Now, Pete the Prayer Plant, that's truly inspired.

JCEDITS

I also have Fergus the Ficus, Harrison the Haworthia, and Henry the Hoya.

PLANTSGUY95

Stop it, now you're just teasing.

JCEDITS

What? I like alliteration.

PLANTSGUY95

What about those secret plants you've been raising all by yourself?

Amanda and Archibald the Aloes?

JCEDITS

No, Artemis and Apollo.

At the totally unexpected leap from his heart her response elicited, Lucas threw his phone down onto the table. JCEdits, whoever and wherever she was in the world, was freaking adorable.

FOUR

Juliet was on her way to the book sale and having an intense back and forth with Charlotte about Plantsguy95, who they'd been discussing at regular intervals since about a week after Juliet had first messaged him. The mystery of his identity was a topic that had come up more than once over the last few months.

Living on opposite sides of the country, Juliet and Charlotte had only met up in person twice since the conference they'd both attended years ago, but that hadn't diminished the friendship. Juliet often thought it made it easier, really, to have her so far away. Then there was no question about having her come over for drinks on a Friday and then have her cancel last minute or steal her boyfriend or any of the other countless ways that in-person friends could let you down.

Though, to be fair, the stealing of the boyfriend was probably a one-off from a particularly bad friend Juliet didn't like to think about, anymore than she liked to think about The Ex. She'd banished both of their names from her vocabulary, editing them completely out of her life, even if what they'd done would always be with her.

Today wasn't about them. Today was about Plantsguy95, and Charlotte was sharing her thoughts yet again on why Juliet should just ask him more personal questions.

EDITSALOTTIE

Since I live in Hollywood, does that mean I'm not in real life?

JCEDITS

Lol, nope. You are a figment of my imagination.

EDITSALOTTIE

Awesome, I guess that means I don't have to finish editing this electrical engineering textbook, do I?

JCEDITS

Thank you again for taking that client.

I just couldn't do another textbook. I needed a break.

EDITSALOTTIE

I get it. Besides, you need to keep your calendar open for a project with BOC potential.

Juliet shook her head and tucked away her phone as she walked onto the library's lawn. With the word count requirements of the BOC awards, she'd have to start something within the next few days if she wanted to be finished by the deadline to submit in a few weeks.

There was nothing she could do about that today, however, so she focused her energy on helping Denise and the Friends get everything setup. The used book sales were always popular, but this one was going to be their biggest ever, thanks to Maude's books. Even before their official start time of nine a.m., there were cars pulling into the parking lot and curious bookworms pacing around the edge of the lawn.

It took a lot of restraint for Juliet to not dive into browsing for herself. In the aftermath of the breakup she'd had to leave behind a lot of books, and it was only now, after almost a year, that her shelves were starting to fill up again with dogeared and highlighted pages. Social media could keep their shiny new covers and unbroken spines. Nothing was as beautiful to Juliet as a well-loved, used book.

With the endless rows of long tables fully loaded and ready to go, Juliet took up her post behind the cash box with Stephen, and gave him a small smile, which, unsurprisingly, he did not return. He did hand her a cookie from the bake sale table though.

The morning passed in a flurry of sales, interspersed with what passed as conversation with Stephen. All Juliet really had to do was nod and say "huh" as he grumbled about the weather, the crowd, and the amount of people using credit cards instead of cash. Two hours later, Denise breezed by to tell them that they'd already surpassed their yearly fundraising target.

Two hours in a crowd was more than enough for Juliet.

"I'm taking a break. I'll be back in fifteen. Can I bring you anything?"

She interpreted Stephen's grunt in response as a no.

Despite Stephen's earlier complaints, the weather was a

perfect early May afternoon with clear blue skies and just a hint of a cool breeze to keep it from getting unbearable. It was a perfect day for gardening, and the plant sale was happening down the street. With the Friends moving up their book sale, Juliet hadn't been able to bring Pete the Prayer Plant like she'd planned. Since the Friends were taking over the house, she wasn't sure if the garden club had a new place to hold a meeting. Unease churned in her stomach as she worried that Pete would never get an in-person diagnosis.

It doesn't matter, she told herself. *He's just a plant, after all.*

And yet, if that were the case, she wouldn't have named him, would she? It was silly, but she did like having them around the house. And not just because it kept her mother happy to know she wasn't living in a "plain, empty box of an apartment" as she'd called Juliet's new place when she'd first moved in.

As Juliet made her way down the street to the small open lot in front of the town hall, she passed at least twenty people, their arms loaded with huge pots overflowing with leaves and blooms. In the other direction, people streamed past with paper bags stuffed to the brim with books. There didn't seem to be many in town who had both plants and books.

Oh, for the love of the Oxford comma. It took her entire amount of self-control to not roll her eyes at the clear division among Greenhaven residents.

In movies and books, small town battles were hilarious. In real life, she spent way too much time listening to her mother complain about whichever committee had made whatever change that pissed off some other group. Greenhaven was too big to have people be that petty, and it was part of why she'd looked at a bigger town rather than move back to her small hometown where her mom still lived. Here in Greenhaven, Juliet was just one of many and she didn't have to pick sides.

It was entirely possible that the town was big enough that there was a distinct and separate book-loving population and plant-loving population. Since she liked both, it put Juliet in the middle yet again, not really a part of anything. It was a familiar, safe place for her to be, even if it was a little lonely to be in the middle.

The entire lot was roped off except for one small entrance. This controlled the flow of people to avoid anyone running off without paying. Juliet made a note to mention it to Denise for the next book sale. The open table layout they were using today made things chaotic, and Juliet was sure there were a decent number of books being put directly into bags without stopping by the cash desk first—and not just because people wanted to avoid dealing with Stephen the grump.

Once she was inside the roped-off area, it was like stepping into a greenhouse. Everywhere she looked, tall leafy plants waved in the breeze, while people discussed the merits of a rubber fig versus a weeping fig and if it was better to plant wisteria in full or partial sun. It was soothing in an unexpected way. The smell of moist earth invaded her nose, and she took a few deep breaths with her eyes closed.

It wasn't quite as good as the smell of old books, but it was pretty close. Pete could do with a few new friends. She checked her watch. There was enough time to get a plant or two and quickly drop them off at home before heading back to the book sale.

There was plenty to choose from. It would have been overwhelming, but she'd learned enough from Plantsguy95 and her own research that there were only a few kinds of plants that worked with both her apartment's sunlight and her lifestyle. Or, in other words, which plants could survive with a lot of sun and being alternately ignored and doted on by Juliet. Succulents and palms made up most of her collection, with the exception of Fergus and Pete.

While she knew she should head toward the cacti, her feet led her straight to the table full of prayer plants. It was something about their open leaves closing up overnight that just made them seem more alive than other plants. Their vitality was irresistible.

Plus, she just really liked how most of them were purple.

A man and a woman, identifiable as garden club volunteers by their aprons with the stencil of the logo over the front pocket, were stationed behind the table. Juliet adeptly avoided their eyes and gave them a polite smile before stooping to examine the plants closer.

"It's really unbelievable," the man's not-very-quiet whisper floated over the leaves. "They've known for months about the plant sale. Months. They couldn't have picked any other weekend to have their book sale?"

The back of Juliet's neck prickled.

"The weather is great. I'm sure they just wanted to avoid the unbearable heat later in the summer," said the woman.

"The parking situation is terrible in this part of town. Everyone knows people use the library's lot for the plant sales because it's closest. But it's full of book people today."

The harsh tone of the man's voice caught Juliet by surprise. It stirred something in her she hadn't felt before, something that could have maybe been loyalty if she'd squinted at it in the right light. With her face still pointed toward the tags on the plants, she let her eyes slide over to the two garden club members.

The one complaining was, of course, gorgeous. His shaggy, light-brown hair was giving off major Indiana Jones vibes with his brown fedora, scruffy, sunburnt cheeks, and cargo shorts filled with tools. Juliet couldn't tell from this angle, but she bet he had those same Harrison Ford blue-green eyes. A tattoo peeked out from the collar of his shirt, and another wrapped around his insanely muscled forearm, both some kind of plant. The delicious nerdiness of someone in the garden club having plant tattoos was almost too much for Juliet. Without thinking, she ran her fingers over her wrist, where her favorite quote was inked.

All attraction to this man evaporated, however, the longer he talked. "It's bad enough they stole the house from us. This is our biggest fundraising day, and now they're stealing all the people."

A burst of indignation flooded into Juliet's mouth, hot and salty. Did he not notice her Friends t-shirt? He must be saying all this just to irritate her. The Friends hadn't asked for Maude Periwinkle to give them her house, she wanted to tell him. Abandoning her intense need for neutrality in small town wars, she straightened up, suddenly eager to stand up for the Friends.

"I'm pretty sure people can like both books and plants, Lucas."

The red-haired woman he was talking to must have been his girlfriend or wife. She was rolling her green eyes in the patiently irritated way that Juliet had overused herself once upon a time. This was clearly something Lucas had been moaning about for weeks and this woman had been putting up with for just as long.

"Are you finding everything ok?"

Juliet took a startled step back when the woman she was not-so-discreetly eavesdropping on spoke to her.

"Yes, I was looking at these prayer plants." Juliet cleared her throat and held one up as if to say, *see, I'm here to give you money, not listen in on your husband's hatred for the library.* "I have one at home and—"

"Do you need some tips on care?" Lucas, the tattooed Indiana Jones, leaned over the table to look directly in Juliet's eyes. "Overwatering is easy with these plants."

Flush and hang. They weren't blue-green like she'd thought. They were an intense brown, rich and complex with flecks of light like the soil in the pot in her hands.

The interest and sincerity in them made her want to punch him in the face. He liked her well enough when she was interested in plants. What would he say if he knew she'd spent her morning at the book sale?

Juliet's newfound loyalty, however, petered out at the thought of public confrontation. She settled for narrowing her eyes and giving her haughtiest sniff, even if to her ears it just sounded like she was allergic to all the pollen floating around in the air.

"I know how to take care of them."

He tsked. "See, people think they know how, but really, it's all about the moisture. You have to—"

"Keep the soil consistently moist and spritz the leaves several times a day." The words poured out of Juliet in a harsher tone than she'd intended. Seeing his surprised face, however, encouraged her to keep going in her recital of all the things her online plant guru had told her. "Fertilize every few weeks spring through fall, keep in indirect sunlight, and repot when the roots start to poke through those little holes in the bottom of the pot."

His wife's lips quirked up a bit. "Looks like she'll do just fine."

Lucas leaned even closer to her across the table and raised his eyebrows. "Those holes on the bottom are called drainage holes, you know."

Heat crept up Juliet's cheeks and she swallowed thickly. "Thanks. I did know that."

"Sounds like you know a lot."

The words were a compliment, but the tone was almost disappointed. Like he'd been looking forward to telling her everything he knew about plants.

Well, looks like he wasn't as useful as he thought he was. It might not have been the defense of the Friends she'd intended, but she'd still managed to put him in his place in her own small way.

Behind the table, the woman shoved Lucas with her hip, and he straightened up with a wink and a smile at Juliet.

"Thanks for stopping by," she said with a quick glance at Lucas. It looked like she was holding back a laugh. "Follow the blue arrows to the register. Be sure to enter the raffle on your way out."

Buoyed by a new and unique mix of adrenaline and loyalty, Juliet smiled back at the woman, looked Lucas up and down in what she hoped was a withering way and not like she was drooling over someone else's husband, and turned away with her new plant in hand.

Lucas had done something wrong, and he wasn't sure what. Sage wouldn't tell him, just shook her head and laughed as the beautiful woman who knew a lot about plants walked away from him with irritation radiating off her like the sun on a parking lot in summer.

"What's so funny?"

The two cousins both turned to see their grandmother standing behind them, her wispy white hair done up in two thin braids looped around her head. This was the first event she'd been to in months, and Lucas was thrilled to see her out and about, even though his heart squeezed to see how heavily she leaned on her cane.

"Lucas was just being his usual know-it-all self, and someone wasn't putting up with it." Sage smirked when Lucas stuck his tongue out at her.

"Behave you two, you're almost forty, for heaven's sake." Granny swatted at their arms before turning her gaze to the retreating figure of the woman, her reddish-brown head bobbing between the tall trees lining the alley to the cashier. "All I saw was Lucas flirting with the lovely young library lady."

"I wasn't flirting." Lucas reached up to cover his face with his hands but stopped and peered at his grandmother. "What do you mean, 'library lady'?"

"She's helping out the Friends with the book sale."

"How do you know?"

Granny arched a feathery white eyebrow. "She's wearing a t-shirt with their logo on it."

"Oh." His mouth pulled down in a frown. "I didn't notice."

Sage snorted. "Yeah, because you were flirting with her."

"That's not possible. I don't flirt." There was no point, not with anyone in town. Not with anyone he'd have to see everywhere when he became too much of a disappointment for them.

"Yeah, just like you don't cry at every *Bachelor* finale."

He inhaled deeply through his nose and reminded himself he loved his family more than his own life.

That didn't mean he had to like them all the time.

"I was trying to help someone, and she wasn't entirely receptive to that help." Lucas glared at them from beneath the brim of his hat. "I wasn't flirting."

"It's all right, dear." His grandmother patted his arm with one hand, then waved to someone passing in front of their table. "We know you're just passionate about pretty . . . plants."

"That's a very polite way of saying he's an asshole, Granny." Sage snickered.

"I prefer to think of it as coming off a bit too strong," Lucas said.

"How can you be so eloquent online, and such a turd in person?"

"I've been getting someone to look over my posts. Can't say you've been as helpful to keep me from being a turd in person."

"All my nudging and eye rolls weren't a big enough hint?" Sage paused, then turned to stare. "Wait, who's looking over your posts? Not that JC editing person you keep mentioning?"

He pushed his hat lower over his eyes and stared out into the crowd milling around. "I don't mention her that much."

The look from his cousin left no doubt he did, in fact, talk about this mysterious online woman quite a bit.

"What's the difference between talking to her online and with someone in person?"

"When someone stands in front of me, asking about plants" —especially someone with hair the color of terracotta and eyes the bright green of a neon pothos—"my words get all mixed up and come out in the wrong tone. Online, I can think about things a bit more."

"To be fair, she hadn't actually asked. She'd just mentioned she had a prayer plant at home, and you launched into an explanation, assuming she knew nothing about it."

"Well most people don't."

"She seemed like she knew what she was talking about." Sage grinned. "I bet she reads a lot."

"Don't get me started on the library people again. Did you make your call to the mayor already?" Lucas had gotten all of his cousins to agree to pass on some "community feedback" to the city. It was all part of his five-step plan to get the house back.

Step one, make sure the mayor knew people were unhappy about it.

Step two through five were still germinating, but once they took root, nothing would put him off course.

Sage sighed. "Yes, though I don't think it'll make a difference. Maude left the house to the Friends, she didn't mention the club at all, end of story."

"Speaking of the Friends, that's why I came over here to find you two." Granny looked up at both of them with eager eyes. "Denise came by earlier to let me know they're going to start cleaning out the house next week, and she thought we might like someone from the club there in case there were things we want to keep."

"How generous of her." Lucas let the sarcasm lay heavy.

"It *is* generous." Granny gave him one of her looks. "Technically, the entire contents of the house also belong to the Friends now. Maude had some very valuable historical botanical drawings that I'm sure they could sell for a lot of money."

"She can't sell them. They're priceless."

"That's not up to us to decide, Lucas." Granny was using her no-nonsense voice that hadn't changed since he and his cousins had been sneaking cookies from the kitchen as kids. "For now, I just need one of you lot to go over there with Stephen Liu a few times next week. You remember him, he used to teach at the high school."

"Definitely not me." Lucas shook his head so vigorously, his hat threatened to fall off. "I want nothing to do with those sneaky swindlers."

"Except maybe one volunteer who likes prayer plants?"

Lucas glared at Sage, who'd already turned back to shake her head at their grandmother.

"I'm sorry, Granny, I like Stephen a lot, but we're just about to head into finals week. I'll have a ton of grading to do."

"What about Oliver?"

"On vacation with his new girlfriend."

"And Mari?"

As they made their way down the long list of cousins, Lucas sighed. None of the other garden club ladies were available, or Granny wouldn't be asking the family to help. There was an order to these kinds of things, a routine that had repeated itself countless times over the years. He knew what was coming, but that didn't make it any easier to hear.

"Lucas, it sounds like you're the only one." Granny peered up at him, her crinkly hazel eyes full of emotion. "Please, would you do this for me?"

When she said it like that, when she looked at him like that, how could he say no?

"Fine. But tell Stephen he'd better bring donuts. They don't deserve your baking for taking the club's house."

"Thank you, my dear." With an affectionate pat on his arm, she drifted off, pulled into a conversation with someone about orchids. "He'll be there Tuesday at eleven. Don't be late."

As frustrated as he was for being dragged into what would surely be a physically and emotionally taxing chore, at least it gave him an idea for step two in his plan. Maude had been a collector, not just of historical horticultural tomes, but also an avid journaler. There might be some clue in her journals to why she'd taken the totally random decision to gift the house to the Friends . . . or proof that she'd been coerced or tricked in some way.

He smiled at Granny, leaning on her cane, now feeling much more certain he'd be able to get back what had been taken from her, from all of them.

"I promise I'll be there."

FIVE

The walk home was longer than expected. It wasn't because the prayer plant was heavy, but because every two feet, someone stopped her to tell Juliet how beautiful it was.

It was a new experience, to have people in Greenhaven make polite conversation as they passed her on the street. It wasn't entirely disagreeable, but when a ten-minute walk turned into twenty, irritation trickled across her skin. Her answers grew clipped and annoyed, and she was worried if there hadn't been any animosity between the garden club and the Friends before, there would be now. Denise was likely getting reports of a book sale volunteer being rude to people up and down Main Street.

By the time she got back to the book sale, almost an hour had passed. Stephen was nowhere to be found, and Denise was there instead, looking frazzled and overwhelmed.

"I'm so sorry, I got held up."

Denise waved a hand. "It's fine. You would not believe what happened while you were gone."

Oh no, more petty gossip. Juliet had had her fill for the day, but Denise looked so expectant, what other choice did she have but to ask, "Oh?"

"Stephen collapsed."

A sharp pang hit Juliet's chest. "Is he okay?" Hot, sticky guilt dripped through her veins. Instead of being here to help, she'd been caught up with Lucas, the library-hating, prayer plant know-it-all with the irritatingly gorgeous brown eyes.

"Yes, yes, his husband came to pick him up."

Denise smiled at a group of people who approached the table, their arms full of books. In an instant, she switched into customer service mode, smiling and making small talk. Apparently, Denise's daughter babysat one man's children, and was on the swim team with someone else's son. All Juliet could contribute to the conversations was at the end, thanking them for supporting the library.

When the last customer walked away, Denise turned back to Juliet. "He'll be ok, but that's not what people will ask you about all afternoon, so you need to know."

Unease creeped along Juliet's skin. While she didn't like gossip, this was the most the president of the Friends had ever spoken to her. The pull of being privy to whatever details she wanted to share was too tantalizing to resist.

"What happened?"

"While everyone was crowded around Stephen, someone tried to steal the cash box." Denise's eyes shone.

Juliet looked down at the intact cash box on the folding table they were standing behind. "Well, it's here now, safe and sound."

"The guy dropped it when he saw people chasing him. It was so odd. Nothing like this has ever happened before at a book sale, so people will be talking about it for a while."

Nerves fluttered in her chest as Juliet thought about the endless loop of gossip that this could lead to. Her mother still talked about the time a few teens had stolen twenty dollars and a case of beer from the small convenience store in her town. Twenty-five years ago.

Unsure how to respond to Denise, Juliet suddenly remembered the setup that the garden club had down the street. "You know, if we set things up like the plant sale, with the ropes and a single entrance—"

"Please don't mention them right now." With two fingers on her temples, Denise rubbed her head. "I've been hearing all morning how annoyed they are with us about moving the book sale."

"Hearing from who?"

Denise rolled her eyes. "Everyone. I had to go over there and talk to their president, Mrs. Geis. We reached an agreement that should keep everyone happy."

Except Denise didn't look or sound very happy about it, which was unusual from what Juliet knew of her.

Juliet took a guess. "Are we stopping the book sale early?"

"No, too late for that. I meant about the house. That's what they're really upset about, after all. The mayor told me she's gotten at least fifteen different calls demanding to know what I did to convince Maude Periwinkle to give us her house."

There was a touch of a tremble in Denise's voice at that, like she was holding back tears. "I never asked her for it. I have no idea why she gave it to the Friends. I've known Mrs. Geis for years, and my grandfather always spoke well of her. She's sweet, but the rest of the garden club is being so unreasonable."

"They certainly are."

Denise smiled at that, and Juliet smiled back, a surge of pride hitting her at this newfound support for the Friends. Then she directed her smile at a woman who'd laid a stack of paperback romances on the table, took her ten dollars, and turned back to Denise. "What's the agreement you made with Mrs. Geis?"

Denise didn't answer her right away but took the time to exclaim over the woman's book choices and offered a reading order for her selection. It wasn't the one Juliet would have recommended, having also read those particular books, but she didn't want to contradict Denise and break whatever tenuous bond was starting to form. The woman walked away smiling, but Denise was frowning when she looked at Juliet.

"Someone from the garden club will be there while we clean out the house, so they can take whatever plant-related books or papers may be there." The furrow between Denise's eyebrows deepened. "Of course, most of the books and papers of Maude Periwinkle will be about plants, so whoever is there with them will have to make sure they don't try to just shove everything in sight into a box and leave with it."

"What do you mean, 'whoever' is there?" Juliet frowned. "I thought Stephen volunteered to clean it out."

The women paused their conversation again as a rush of people arrived to pay for their books. The tables that had been piled high that morning with books were now looking much sparser. Juliet felt another rush of pride to think of how many scholarships and activities the Friends would be able to fund over the next six months.

First loyalty, then guilt, now pride. This day was turning out to be a lot more emotional than Juliet had anticipated.

When Denise turned to her once the table was clear of customers, however, a much less positive feeling rippled through Juliet. Anxiety mixed with a familiar, unavoidable dread. Denise had the same expression as when Juliet's mother asked her to come visit.

"Stephen did volunteer, but that was before his episode this afternoon." Denise tidied the free bookmarks and stickers on the table. "His husband said it was a flare up of his chronic autoimmune disorder. He'll be taking it easy for the next few weeks."

A jolt of bittersweet recognition hit Juliet. Her father had had an autoimmune disorder. There was no reason for Stephen to have told her, but it did make her feel less guilty about stepping away for so long earlier. She knew those kinds of things were tricky, and it wasn't because he'd been at the cash table on his own for an hour that he'd collapsed. Still, she wished she'd been there. Any kind of episode was uncomfortable and unsettling, and she'd gotten good at reassuring her father before he'd passed.

"I'll need a new volunteer."

It wasn't a question, but Juliet already knew what she wanted to say. "No" was a complete sentence, as all the various women-led business accounts she followed online liked to remind her via inspirational memes.

And yet.

She was between gigs, and her week stretched empty before her. There was only so much social media post planning she could do, and she was already a few weeks ahead of her posting schedule.

A deep, resounding gong of duty rang inside of Juliet. It wasn't quite as strong as the one that didn't allow her to let more than two calls in a row from her mother go to voicemail, but it was close. Juliet might not be truly a part of this town, she might not know as many people as Denise, but she could do this. She could help the Friends in this small way.

Before she could say anything, Denise kept going. "It's been a day of bad news. Our regular editor just let me know she had a family emergency, and she won't be able to make the printer's deadline." The older woman looked earnestly into Juliet's eyes. "I'd be willing to pay double your regular rate for some work on the library's literary magazine."

There was no way Juliet could say no to that. The excitement over a potential BOC entry overwhelmed whatever sense of duty to the Friends had been growing inside of her. Duty to herself came first, after all. It was what had kept her safe the last year.

"I'd love to help with the house and the editing project."

Relief and gratitude lit up Denise's face. "Great. I'll email you all the details once we're done here." She looked around the lawn and chuckled. "Which might be sooner than scheduled. Not much left."

Juliet laughed along with Denise, pleased at how the day was turning out. A new plant, a BOC project, and a small step toward belonging to this town.

She'd be polite but firm with whoever would clean out the house with her, and in a week or two she'd be done. There'd be no need to get involved in whatever drama seemed to be taking root with the garden club.

SIX

PLANTSGUY95

How was the plant sale?

Did you take Pete?

JCEDITS

No, he stayed at home, but I got him a new friend, despite a run in with a Mr. Darcy type.

PLANTSGUY95

Mr. Darcy? Is he like Mr. Bean?

JCEDITS

Um, that's a joke, right?

I can't always tell online . . .

PLANTSGUY95

Just give me a second to Google.

JCEDITS

I can't believe you have to Google Mr. Darcy.

What kind of education are kids getting these days?

PLANTSGUY95

High school was a long time ago, and I wasn't in AP Lit like you obviously were.

JCEDITS

AP Lit and Lang, thank you very much.

PLANTSGUY95

Okay, so in my three seconds of research, it appears that Mr. Darcy is an attractive, rich, asshole who insults people within minutes of meeting them?

JCEDITS

Well, there's more to him than that, but sure.

PLANTSGUY95

You're dying to give me an AP Lit lecture right now, aren't you?

JCEDITS

Fine, no lecture, new subject: it looks like you were also at a plant sale this weekend?

PLANTSGUY95

Yeah, it's that season. I saw signs for about five in my area alone for the same day.

We raised a lot of money for our club.

JCEDITS

What do garden clubs do?

Besides sell plants and help people like me from killing them?

PLANTSGUY95

How much time do you have? Lol.

JCEDITS

They do that much, huh?

Lucas stopped in the middle of the sidewalk to think about how to answer JC. He was already late in meeting Sage at her house to help her plant some Creeping Phlox along the borders of the path leading to her house. Though he suspected what she really wanted to do was convince him to stop his campaign against the Friends before he'd gotten too far.

The calls he'd made to Mayor Taylor had been, well, less than eloquent in the delivery of his message. At least online he could write, delete, and rewrite until he'd figured out the best way to give a little information without overwhelming anybody.

His posts from the weekend had been about how local garden clubs were a great resource for those looking to learn about plants and environmental responsibility. Now, for JC, he added details on how the club helped the community at large, and the big native plants movement Lucas was particularly keen to bring awareness to, even if it was just in his small corner of the internet.

It presented in a much more streamlined and thoughtful way than he tended to do in person, as his failed interaction this weekend with the woman from the book sale had proven. Though his urge to impress "the lovely library lady," as Granny has called her, might have had more to do with her intense eyes than he'd ever willingly admit to his cousin.

Just as he got to Sage's house, JC replied.

JCEDITS

So it's not just sitting around in someone's garden sipping tea?

PLANTSGUY95

Oh, we do some of that, too.

Are you thinking of joining your local club?

These kinds of organizations are always looking for volunteers.

JCEDITS

I have another group I support, I don't want to
spread myself too thin.

PLANTSGUY95

I could make a terrible plant joke, but I won't.

JCEDITS

I'll take all the jokes I can get this week.

PLANTSGUY95

Did something happen with a client?

JC didn't share many stories about her work, but he knew
from other friends that the self-employed life had its ups and
downs. He could usually tell when things were slow, since she
would post more often and run half-price deals on her services.

JCEDITS

No, not a client, just the group I'm in needs me
for a big project the next week or two.

It's an awkward situation and I don't want to be
in the middle, but I think I can really help.

PLANTSGUY95

That was extremely vague, lol, but you help a
lot of people so I'm sure you'll do fine.

JCEDITS

By "help a lot of people," do you mean I help
you avoid embarrassing typos in your posts?

PLANTSGUY95

You'll still have time for that, won't you?

I'm doing a whole series on corncockles and
pussytoes and I just know I'm going to get
myself into trouble.

For the hundredth time, Lucas reminded himself that this was all online. This wasn't real. Well, she was a real person, obviously. Or perhaps the most advanced bot on the planet. But either way, bot or human, this was just a friendship. He had other online friends, other plant accounts that he traded articles and tips with. JC was just like them.

Maybe if he said it enough, he'd actually start to believe it.

"You can't just say something enough and people will believe it, Lucas."

Sage pointed her spade at his head.

"I am a citizen of this town. I have a right to talk to the mayor if I'm concerned." He dug his trowel into the pile of dirt in front of him and lifted. "She should know how people in the town feel about this."

"The Friends have done nothing wrong. The plant sale made more money than last year, probably because of all the extra foot traffic from the book sale. We'll find another place for our meetings." Sage was doing that thing where she was being reasonable, which Lucas totally didn't appreciate. The dirt in Lucas's trowel went onto the pile beside him.

"There are decades of memories there, for the club, for Granny, for our family." He shook his head. "And we're expected to just grab a few tokens and that's it? What about all her plants?"

"What about them?"

"She spent years collecting those, getting their placement

right, rotating them as the sun changed during the year. Are the library people going to take care of them?"

"I'm sure they can figure it out."

"Well, the club gave her those calamondin orange trees. We should at least get those back."

"You're abnormally fixated on this, even for you." Her eyes were focused on digging the hole in front of her, not on Lucas, but her words cut into him anyway. "The Friends of the Library are an organization who helps the town, just like we are. They need a space to meet, to store their stuff. Why does it matter who actually owns or uses the house?"

"It matters." Dirt went flying when he shoved his trowel into the hole with the irritation coursing through his blood. "Maude was Granny's best friend. There's no way she's happy about never being in the house again."

"So then have her come with you on Tuesday to sort through everything."

"If she could do it herself, she wouldn't have asked me." Lucas knew that the club was everything to Granny, and it was physically getting harder for her to participate. The plant sale had worn her out for days. Everything she loved was being taken away from her. "I'll get back what should be hers."

"She didn't ask you to get the house back, did she? She just wants you to help the Friends clean it out. Get whatever mementos you think she'd like most from Maude's things."

It was time to share step two of his plan with Sage.

"While I'm cleaning, I'm going to try to find something in Maude's papers that proves she didn't mean to give the Friends her house. It has to be a mistake."

There was a long, drawn-out sigh from his cousin. It was a sigh he'd heard many times before, whenever he'd set his mind to something and fought his hardest to get it. Most of his cousins called it his "congenital stubbornness." "Being an annoying pain in the ass" was what Sage usually called it.

She put her trowel on the ground and wiped her forehead. "I know I can't talk you out of this, but can I at least give you some advice?"

"Always."

"Remember, it isn't Stephen's fault he's there to clean things out. He's a good guy. I worked with him at the school, even if you don't remember him. He's not some evil corporation coming to take everything away from you and your loved ones. He's a person, just like you."

Lucas rolled his eyes. "Don't worry, I'll be polite."

She threw her gardening gloves at him. "Good, because if you're not, Granny will hear about it."

Tuesday at eleven, Lucas was waiting in front of Maude's house, a Tupperware full of Granny's famous—at least in Greenhaven —baked goods. Because of course she'd made some. Stephen Liu had better appreciate them.

Except it wasn't Stephen who he saw walking down the street toward the house. It was the woman from the plant sale, the one with the terracotta hair and neon-green eyes. The one who, when she noticed Lucas, stopped in her tracks halfway across the street.

Once the initial shiver of anticipation made its way down Lucas's back, he noticed the tight purse of her lips and narrowed eyes.

Squaring his shoulders, Lucas reminded himself that he was there to do one job, and that was to protect the interests of the garden club. He'd scour every single piece of paper inside the house to make sure there wasn't a second will or blackmail letter that changed everything. He'd carry every single one of the plants inside back to his house two miles away if he had to, just to be sure they didn't die.

He didn't want to like her, didn't want to find anything attractive or pleasant about her. So what if she talked about plants like she knew more than he did, and her hair was doing that swishy thing around her face he liked so much.

She was the enemy.

His cousin's voice popped into his head, reminding him that she was just another person. Even if she wasn't Stephen, that didn't change Sage's advice.

Unfortunately, the hot mix of attraction and irritation running through Lucas's veins right now was not able to listen to advice.

Was it immature for him to dislike her because his family had teased him about flirting with her? Probably.

Had he been a bit of a jerky know-it-all when they'd first met? Possibly.

Was he going to attempt to change her first impression of him? Definitely not.

This was about more than whatever inkling of attraction he'd felt. Who cared if it was the first time in forever that his jaded and bitter heart had been even somewhat attracted to someone. It didn't mean anything. This was about protecting the garden club and his family.

And this woman, whoever she was, wasn't a part of either group.

SEVEN

Of course it was him. And of course he looked even better than he had Saturday at the plant sale. The hat was gone, and his wavy brown hair fell slightly below his ears, the perfect length to run her hands through. Juliet had a weakness for guys with long hair.

Which, based on her experience, meant Lucas was the last person she should be interested in. Only a fool attempted the same formula twice and expected different outcomes. Men like Lucas were her kryptonite, and she had to stay away.

Luckily, if the sour expression on his face was any indication, Juliet wouldn't have that hard of a time keeping her distance.

"You're not Stephen Liu." A muscle in his jaw twitched. "Disappointed?"

Woah, where had that sassy tone come from? Juliet tried to hide her surprise, and then her delight at how her comeback had destabilized him. He narrowed his eyes, then nodded once, like he was having an internal argument with himself that he'd just won.

He stuck out his hand, his tattoo on full display. "Lucas Geis."

She ignored his hands, keeping her arms folded across her chest. Touching him would be a terrible idea. "Juliet Chapman. Are you related to Mrs. Geis, the president of the garden club?"

"She's my grandmother." There was a long pause, then he held out a Tupperware, slowly, like he didn't want to part with it. "She made us cookies."

"Well, at least one Geis is polite."

Juliet didn't know who had taken over her mouth. This was the outpouring of spontaneous snark she admired in movies or read in books. She bit her lip, fighting the urge to apologize, to take it back.

He ran the hand not holding the cookies through his glorious hair. "I'm sorry if I was a little . . . presumptuous this weekend. I'm used to people coming to the plant sales without any idea what they're doing."

That wasn't technically apologizing, but Juliet had reached her boldness limit for the day it seemed. Rather than accept or reject his semi-apology, she simply changed the subject. "We should get started. How long can you stay today?"

He blinked a few times, as if thrown by her sudden businesslike tone. "I don't have to be at work until three today. I'm closing the store."

Juliet reached into her bag for the keys, so she wasn't looking at him when she asked, "What store?"

The only reason she wanted to know was to avoid it.

"The hardware store."

Keys in hand, she made her way up the walkway and the porch stairs. "The one on Elm?"

"That's the one." He waited on the lawn while she opened the door. "Where do you work?"

Despite almost ten years of working for herself, this was always a hard question for Juliet. Even before The Ex had given her work as a reason for the breakup—one of the fifty-two he'd recited that horrible day—she'd always felt like it made her different from everyone else. Of course she knew tons of other editors online who were doing the same thing, but they also seemed to have a life outside of work. They were either parents fitting in editing around school pick ups and bedtimes, or part of a stylish remote-working couple who traveled all over the world together. Juliet just had work. And now this house cleaning project.

Instead of answering the question, Juliet stepped into the house and let out a little breath of surprise. "Wow, this place is beautiful."

The thump of Lucas's feet on the steps told her he was right behind her. She moved aside to let him pass. With an ease that Juliet only felt in her mother's house, Lucas walked through the grand front foyer and through a door at the end of the hallway.

"I'll put the cookies in the kitchen if you want them later."

"Don't you want any?"

He reappeared, a slight smile on his face. "I can get them whenever I want."

Her stomach swooped downward. It probably wasn't intended as innuendo, but that's all Juliet could hear.

She cleared her throat and pulled out a clipboard from her bag. "Why don't we do an initial tour of the building and see what's in store for us. Denise left me notes but they're pretty vague."

He nodded, and she let out a little internal sigh of relief. Maybe this wouldn't be that bad.

"Anything of interest in the kitchen?"

"Besides the cookies?"

Her heart gave a traitorous thump against her rib cage as she narrowed her gaze on him. "Yes, besides the cookies."

"There are a few herbs on the windowsill I can take with me today."

Juliet made a note on her clipboard. "The Friends can handle any plants that are here."

Lucas scoffed, a little half-chuckle half-snort.

"I believe that *you* know how to take care of them." His emphasis on the word you, and the way he stared right into her eyes was so intense, Juliet had to turn away.

What was his deal? Was he trying to distract her so he could run off with whatever he wanted?

No, she had to focus. Denise was counting on her to uphold the interests of the Friends, and that meant keeping as much as possible, even the plants.

"There was nothing calling out the plants in the will." She looked down at the clipboard with Denise's notes. "Technically, everything belongs to us—er, to the Friends, that is."

Juliet could feel the heat of a blush rush across her face. There was that "us" word again, that Lucas seemed to bring out in her thinking, pitting her against him and the "them" of the garden club.

This was about Juliet's career, though, not whatever petty political machinations were happening in Greenhaven. The BOC award might finally be within reach for Juliet, but the first step was getting the actual document to edit. Not wanting to pile too much on Juliet at once, Denise had said she wouldn't send her anything until the house was cleaned out. This was fine with Juliet, since she knew once she got started on the project, she likely wouldn't come up for air for days. The sooner the house was clear, the sooner her real work could start.

"The library wants the plants?" Lucas crossed his arms across his wide chest. The muscles beneath his t-shirt flexed slightly at the movement.

With more effort than expected, she drew her eyes back to

his face. "The Friends are perfectly capable of taking care of a few kitchen herbs. I have some myself at home."

He tilted his head. "What kind?"

"Cilantro, basil, and rosemary." She jutted out her chin proudly. "And before you ask, I grew them all from seed. I didn't buy them fully grown."

His eyebrows shot up and he nodded once. "I'm impressed."

"Now that we've established the kitchen herbs are staying, can we please continue the tour?" She waved her clipboard toward the stairs. "You know this place better than I do. Where should we start?"

Asking him to lead seemed to be the trick to improving his mood. The next half-hour was a slow walk around the house's many rooms, where he happily provided details on the plants, the club, everything and anything he knew. It was a long house, going back deep into the property, with very little actual garden. Maude seemed to have compensated for that with vibrant greenery in every single room, none of which Denise had taken note of. She only cared about the books.

Naturally, Lucas cared a lot about the plants. He listed out their names, and Juliet took careful notes, including their locations.

"We'll probably need to get a service to come in here to take care of them," Juliet said, mostly to herself. "Unless someone from the Friends could come in every day."

"A service?" Lucas sounded horrified. "All they'll do is charge you a fortune to dump a bunch of water on them twice a week."

Juliet clicked her tongue, biting back the urge to stick it out at him. "I said *probably*."

"The garden club can keep taking care of them, just like we have since Maude went into the long-term care facility last year."

"Can I ask what happened to her?" Holding the clipboard at her side, Juliet looked up at him standing underneath an enormous micans plant with tendrils so long they brushed his shoulders. "If that's okay? I don't want to pry. It's just . . . I haven't lived here that long, so I don't know what the story is."

There had to be a story, but there was zero chance of Juliet finding out on her own. People didn't share things with her, they didn't open up. Not the way they seemed to do with others. It was like people could tell from something in her face that she didn't belong.

Lucas stepped out from under the plant to lean against the doorframe and crossed his arms. "It's not a secret. She got cancer, and since she was in her eighties, she decided it wasn't worth all the pain of chemo and radiation. But then she couldn't keep going up and down the stairs, so she moved out about three months before she died."

"I'm sorry." The sad story was all too familiar to Juliet. "Losing someone is never easy, no matter the circumstances."

The muscle in his jaw twitched again, and he looked down at his feet. "She and my grandmother were best friends."

"You must have spent a lot of time in this house, and not just with the garden club."

He nodded, still not meeting her eyes.

Oh, gapping comma. Did Denise realize that this wasn't just a clubhouse, but someone's home?

It doesn't change anything. Juliet was here to help the Friends, who'd legally been gifted the house. Maude Periwinkle must have had her reasons, and they didn't matter to Juliet.

It was clear they mattered to Lucas, however.

"Why don't we each grab some boxes and start sorting." A change of subject—and some distance—would do them both some good. "If I come across anything of interest, I'll put it aside for you to look at, if you'll do the same?"

"How will you know what's of interest to me?" He narrowed his eyes. "I mean, to the club?"

Juliet bristled and held up her clipboard over her chest like a shield. "If you don't trust me, then we can work in the same room. But it'll take longer. Maybe all week instead of a few days."

The thought of working with him longer shouldn't have sent a rush of eager anticipation through her. Especially since he was looking at her like she was the last person he wanted to spend an afternoon in the same room with.

Then again, Juliet seemed to have a knack for being attracted to people who wanted nothing to do with her.

He put his hands on his hips. "It doesn't matter how long it takes. It matters that it's done right."

"As much as I hate to admit this, I agree with you."

Surprise flickered across his face, lighting up his deep-brown eyes.

Pleased that she'd once again said something unexpected, she held out a cardboard box. "Let's get started."

The next few hours were not the easiest of Juliet's life, but they weren't the worst. Part of her actually enjoyed the careful examination and battle over almost every single item in the upstairs office, where they'd started. It was the smallest room, with most of it already packed away and sent to various relatives across the country.

The concentration and categorization it required was familiar to her, not totally unlike what she did as an editor. It would have been almost soothing, the stillness of a house empty of people, and the smell of leaves and dirt underneath the mustiness of old books. It would have been, if not for the constant interruptions from Lucas.

"What about this book on plant fungus?"

"What about this newspaper article from 1965 about the benefits of compost?"

"No one reads encyclopedias anymore. But these have Maude's notes in the margins. What do you think?"

It was hard to tell if he sought to irritate her on purpose or if he wanted to be as thorough as possible. Sometimes, when there was a pause in his nonstop questions, she'd glance at him and see his head bent over a photo album, a sad smile on his face. He clearly cared about all of this, Maude, the house, the garden club. If it weren't for those brief moments of peace, and the BOC-potential project looming at the end of the week, she'd have called Denise within the first hour to beg her to find anyone else to do this.

Around two in the afternoon, they'd finally finished the room, with only a small box of items going to the garden club. Juliet felt a small sense of victory, knowing she'd done what Denise had asked. She was about to suggest they stop for the day when Lucas's phone rang.

"Hey, Sage, what's up?" He glanced at her quickly, then stepped out into the hallway. His voice drifted away as he thumped down the stairs.

Finally left alone, Juliet wandered into the next room, a spare bedroom full of bookcases. A groan escaped her lips. This room would take twice as long as the office if Lucas kept up his battle over every single book and scrap of paper.

Running her hands along the spines, she closed her eyes and breathed in the smell. It was calming after what had been an unsettling day. She decided to play her favorite game at libraries and bookstores. When she opened her eyes, she picked whatever book her hand was on and read it.

Ten minutes later, she was curled up on a couch, her nose buried so deeply in a book, that she didn't hear Lucas approaching until he was right behind her. She nearly jumped out of her skin when he spoke not two feet from her ear.

"Whatcha reading?"

"Holy Oxford Comma!" Juliet put a hand to her racing heart. A tiny upward tilt of his lip was the only indication he had meant to scare her. The fact that the roguish slant to his mouth made her heart pound even harder was irritating beyond belief. He was too attractive for his own good.

"Not that it matters, but I am pro-oxford comma," he said.

She was as well, and judging from the way his eyes sparkled with barely concealed laughter, he'd probably guessed that about her.

"I'm reading about *Maranta leuconeura.*"

Two lines appeared between his eyebrows. "Prayer plants? Why? You seemed to know what you were doing at the plant sale."

Heat rushed to Juliet's face. She didn't care what he thought of her, but it was still embarrassing to admit her failure to someone in real life. This was why Plantsguy95 was the best. Even if behind his helpful messages he was judging her from wherever he was in the world, she didn't have to see it on his face. However, he'd shared about Maude being sick, so it seemed only fair to reciprocate some vulnerability.

"Mine has been struggling for a while now. I'm not sure what to do."

Interest flickered across his face, the amused sparkle in his eyes now one of excitement and interest. "Did you check the drainage? Have you been misting it with a spray bottle?"

Juliet rolled her eyes. "Of course. I follow tons of plant accounts on social media." Technically a lie, but there was no way she was admitting the truth, that she'd learned everything from someone she didn't know called Plantsguy95. "I did all the things they say to do. I even sent a picture to one."

Lucas was shaking his head. "It's hard to get a sense of something from just a picture. I could take a look, if you want to bring it by the next time we're here to clean."

"Pete doesn't like leaving the house."

"Pete the prayer plant?"

Now the heat had spread to her whole body. She looked down at the book, at the floor, anywhere but at him.

"I know, it's dumb, to name my plants, but they're alive, you know? I just felt weird to have all these living things in my house and just call them 'it.'"

If anyone could understand, it would be someone in the garden club, right? She braved a peek up at him. His furrowed brow and intense expression were not what she'd expected to see, however, and her stomach lurched at his scrutiny.

He must think I'm a total oddball.

Not that she cared, of course.

"I need to go." He stood, brushed invisible dust off his jeans, then flexed his hands like they'd been burned. "I'm sorry, I forgot I—I have to take my grandmother to an appointment before work today."

Without even saying goodbye, he turned on his heels and practically ran from the room, from Juliet and whatever distasteful trait she'd just inadvertently revealed about herself.

The smell of moss and dirt lingered in the air after he rushed out.

EIGHT

Lucas burst into Sage's house without even knocking. He'd practically flown here after work, breaking several local speed ordinances.

"How soon can you get the other cousins here? I am having a bit of a crisis."

Now fully inside, he paused and looked around the living room. All eight of his female cousins were there, wine glasses in hand, with *The Bachelor* blaring on Sage's giant TV.

"Um, is this a bad time?" He took a small step back, away from the sixteen eyes glaring at him.

"If you can wait until after the rose ceremony without saying a single word, then we'll listen to whatever minor inconvenience you feel is destroying your privileged life as a reasonably attractive middle-class white man this week." His youngest cousin Heather was in her second year of college and, as she liked to tell him almost weekly, had zero patience for what she called Lucas's "millennial melodrama."

If he hadn't been in such desperate need for her help, he would have pointed out she was obsessed with a show about a privileged middle-class white man picking his future wife in a public arena. Instead, he toned down the teasing to the bare minimum.

"Only reasonably attractive?"

"Shh," they all said in unison.

Knowing when he was outnumbered—and frankly, just Sage alone would have been enough to keep him in line—he bit back the five hundred questions that came up over the next forty-five minutes of increasingly tense reality television. He'd stopped coming to *Bachelor* night when he started working at the hardware store and his schedule changed, so he hadn't bothered keeping up with the new season. Knowing that commercials were to be used to discuss the contestants, he made himself useful by filling their glasses without asking and heating up some of the frozen potstickers Sage kept in the freezer.

Finally, when all roses had been distributed, and the teary loser sent home to await her triumphant return on *Bachelor in Paradise* next year, all eight cousins turned their attention to Lucas.

"What seems to be the trouble?" Sage said. "Did you find whatever secret paper Maude was hiding that proves the Friends of the Library are terrible, house-stealing vermin?"

The rest of his cousins were smirking. Sage must have updated them on step two of his plan. They'd all made their calls to the mayor to complain as he'd requested. Only a few of the cousins were officially in the club, but it was a big enough part of Granny's life that everyone had an interest in seeing her happy. They'd all spent countless hours at Maude's house growing up, at various parties and events. This was as much a loss for the Geis cousins as it was for Granny.

"Um, not exactly." He ran his hands through his hair, then leaned back on the couch. "So you know that girl I talk to on social media? JC? The editor?"

"The one you mention at least twice a day?" Heather raised

a feathery eyebrow in a very Granny-like way, except hers were dark brown, not white. "Yes, I think we all know about her. Did she finally send you a picture of her face? Does it not live up to the plastic surgery catfishing aesthetic you've grown accustomed to?"

"Did you send her a picture?" Mari snickered and held a hand to her mouth. "Oh, Lucas, not a picture of your . . . plants, I hope. We raised you better than that."

"No. There were no pictures." He stood up, realized there was no space to pace with the eight of them spread out on every available surface, and sat down again. "There was no need. She's here. In Greenhaven. She's the person the Friends sent to clear out the house with me."

"The same woman from the plant sale?"

He nodded.

Their collective gasp was more surprised than when the final rose had gone to Lauren instead of Kristen.

"Did she tell you that?"

He shook his head. "She said something that only JC would know."

"Does she know who you are?"

He hesitated, but shook his head again.

There was another gasp from the group.

Despite the stress coursing through his veins, he couldn't help snorting at their ridiculousness. "If any reality TV producers are walking by, they'd hire you all on the spot. The Greenhaven Geis Gals."

"*Lucas.*" As usual, Sage ignored his teasing to focus on more serious matters, running a hand along the arm of the couch and frowning slightly. "Did you not tell her who you are when you realized who she was?"

"I didn't know what to do. She's this online, imaginary

person, and then she was there in front of me. What would you have done?"

Their responses were so fast they drowned each other out.

"Admitted my crush on her."

"Told her who I was."

"Kissed her."

"Ew, consent much?"

"Given her an obvious hint about who I was."

"'Accidentally' mentioned my social media account."

"Left my phone out so she could 'accidentally' see my account."

He threw his hands up in the air and sank back into the couch cushions.

"Fine, I could have done at least two reasonable things besides run out of there." His face grew hot under the compound weight of his cousins' glares. "I did say I was sorry I had to leave. I'm not a monster."

"Debatable." Heather sniffed indignantly from the depths of the armchair closest to the TV. "You wanted Lauren to get the rose."

It was scary sometimes how easily all of them could read him, even without him saying a word. He'd known all of them since they were born, except Sage. She'd only been four when his parents had fostered him, and five when he'd been officially adopted, but she was still older by three months, which made her the oldest of all the Geis cousins.

While Heather's comment sent them all into another recap of the episode, Lucas hid his face in his hands, not wanting them to see what he was thinking. He didn't even know himself yet. All he knew was that the JC online was funny and sweet, but the Juliet he'd spent the afternoon with was uptight and rigid and horrible.

No, she wasn't horrible. The Friends were. Not them individually, but the organization itself, taking something so important from him and his family. That house held memories of fights and first kisses, of long summer nights hiding from the adults in the upstairs office, of getting lost in the bamboo plants in the back sunroom like it was their own private jungle. What did the Friends have in that house? Nothing at all.

While the Lauren versus Kristen battle raged around him, he took out his phone and scrolled back through the most recent messages with JC—Juliet. He'd been the one to tell her to go to the plant sale, to encourage her to get in touch with the garden club. And she'd done it.

Something must have changed in his expression as an idea flitted through his head, because Sage shushed everyone.

"Oh no, Lucas. What are you thinking?"

"Nothing." Even to his ears, it had come out too quickly to be believable. He sighed, knowing he'd need their input anyway before going forward with his plan. "Just that I haven't given up on getting the house back."

Half of his cousins gave him encouraging nods, the other half shook their heads, including Sage.

"It's too late. The will's been—"

"I know about the will, but the Friends could still decide on their own to give it back, right?"

Sage frowned. "I guess."

"Maybe there's a way that I could encourage Juliet to help the club. She actually likes plants. She's been chatting with Plantsguy95 for months about them. But since she has a terrible first impression of me, Lucas—"

"Which is your own know-it-all fault, you realize?"

Lucas obviously ignored that. "Maybe I could do it as Plantsguy95. Point out all the ways the club helps the town, see if she'd advocate to the president about giving it back. Or at least get her to tell me what their plans are for it, see if I can take that to Mayor Taylor so she'll step in or something."

All eight of them were speechless, which was such a rare occurrence. Lucas was tempted to film it for posterity.

Heather was the first to speak up. "That's a terrible idea. Loathsome."

Mari spoke just a second later. "That's not a bad idea."

Everyone turned to stare at Mari.

"I always knew I liked you best." Lucas smiled.

Mari leaned back on the couch and rolled her eyes. "It's not the best idea you've ever had, but it's far from loathsome. You're not trying to hurt her. It's not like it's her personal house. You just want to help the club, help Granny."

"Exactly. This isn't anything against her."

"Are you sure?" Sage crossed her arms over her chest. "You seemed really annoyed with her at the plant sale when you found out she was part of the Friends. And the texts you sent while you were cleaning this afternoon weren't exactly singing her praises."

"Okay, so there were a few frustrated moments this afternoon when she didn't agree with me about a certain book." More like fifteen, but that was besides the point. "That was before I knew her."

"You mean before you knew she was your secret online crush."

It was hard for him to reconcile the two images he had of her. Though both her in-person and online persona were quippy, there was an edge to her in person that was irritating in a way that he couldn't explain. Her eyes were sharp, like she was taking everything in and categorizing it, judging it. It must be what made her such a good editor.

That same sharpness was what made her the perfect ally for the Friends, rejecting almost every single item he'd put forward as essential for the club to keep. In the end, he'd left with only a tiny box of truly precious personal items. Which—once he calmed down—he'd be willing to admit was more meaningful to Granny than stacks of books with a few scribbles in Maude's messy cursive.

"Well, consider me un-crushed. She's not the same person online."

"Neither are you."

"Yes, but it's not like she cares about who Plantsguy95 is." *Or cares about him*, he added in his head. The smirks from his cousins let him know that thought had been well communicated by his face. "It doesn't matter to her who I am online or off."

Mari nodded. "It's about online brand management. He's not trying to trick anyone."

Sage and Heather still looked unconvinced, but the others were nodding.

"She should know it's you," Heather said, arms crossed so tightly it looked painful.

"I'll tell her, I promise, just not right away. I need to at least try it my way first." Lucas looked around the room. "For Granny."

He would do anything for her, they all would. So they all nodded, though Heather and Sage were giving him the evil eye the entire time.

"You have two weeks," Sage declared with an imperious air. "Then I'll tell her myself who you are."

"No way. There's no way anyone would change their mind that quickly." He glanced at the TV. "Reality TV stars excepted. I need at least three months."

That's how long it had taken from their first quick exchange to build up to their more regular messaging rhythm. It was still sporadic, but it averaged about once or twice a week now. He couldn't suddenly start writing to her every day.

"One month," Sage countered.

"Six weeks."

Heather leaned over to whisper in Sage's ear, and the eldest Geis cousin nodded at Lucas.

That still wasn't a lot of time, but he'd managed to get her ponytail palm thriving in less than that, so there was a good chance he could pull this off.

Knowing this was a very serious deal he was entering into, he stood and went to the counter in the kitchen, where a vase of flowers was always full. He pulled out a single red *Dahlia*, took it back out to the living room, and handed it to Sage. His other cousin—actually named Dahlia—brightened when she saw he'd picked her flower.

"Will you accept this flower as a sign of my commitment?"

Sage grabbed it and smacked him on the arm with it.

He took that as a yes.

NINE

When Lucas was late the next day, Juliet got started on cleaning out the house without him, though it felt like cheating somehow.

The box he'd packed away with some of Maude's more personal items was still in the hallway, where he'd forgotten it after running off the day before.

Having a guy run away from her was nothing new, unfortunately. Even if she didn't particularly like Lucas—his perfect, wavy hair and intense brown eyes excepted—it still hurt. It was still proof that she wasn't even interesting enough for someone to want to spend an afternoon in the same room with her, interacting only out of an obligation to his grandmother.

Though The Ex hadn't run, technically. He'd kept the apartment, after all, and sent her stuff shoved haphazardly in boxes to her mom's house. That had definitely hurt much worse than Lucas making up some random excuse to avoid talking to her all afternoon.

Juliet wandered back into the small, upstairs library that also held a daybed, presumably for guests or mid-afternoon reading naps, and picked up a random book from the shelf. Flipping it open revealed a photo album full of jagged-edged, black-

and-white photos from what must have been the garden club's early days.

There were pages and pages of photos, full of happy, smiling people. There were photos of plants the size of grown women and tiny little cacti held in open palms. There were a few photos of a young Maude and a tall, serious-faced man with glasses. Even in grainy black and white and standing several feet apart, the air sizzled with sparks between the two of them.

Juliet sighed and closed the book. It made sense Lucas would want to fight so hard for the memory of this fun, vibrant woman who'd surrounded herself with men and plants and friends. Maude had been so different from Juliet, who would probably never have another man in her life again, and now only had plants to keep her company.

I have online friends, she reminded herself, and put the photo album in the box in the hallway with the other personal items. *Those absolutely count.*

As if to prove to herself she wasn't alone, she pulled out her phone and looked at her messages. There was one waiting for her from Charlotte, and—her chest hitched when she saw it— another from Plantsguy95. She opened his first.

PLANTSGUY95

How's the big project going with your volunteer group?

The fact that he'd remembered made a wide smile spread across her face. Ok, sure, all he had to do was look up a few lines at their last messages, but still. It was proof that out there in the world, someone was thinking about her. That was the definition of a friend, right?

JCEDITS

So far so good, but the person helping me has abandoned me.

PLANTSGUY95

What a jerk.

And you already had to deal with Mr. Darcy last weekend

JCEDITS

Actually, he's the one helping me.

It's like I'm trapped at Netherfield. At least there's no Caroline Bingley with him.

PLANTSGUY95

Okay, I have no idea what any of that means.

JCEDITS

You would if you read the book.

PLANTSGUY95

Who has time to read?

Besides you.

JCEDITS

There are two movie adaptations.

PLANTSGUY95

That's cheating.

Maybe I'll do an audiobook while I'm gardening.

JCEDITS

That's when I listen to audiobooks, too.

There was a tug at her chest to think someone who might live halfway across the country wasn't that different from her. That they were able to joke about things without her feeling embarrassed afterward the way she always seemed to be when it was in person. The cookie comment to Patrice still came to mind at unexpected moments during the day. She'd need something even more awkward soon to push it out of regular rotation in her over-analysis cycle.

A loud knocking on the door pulled her attention away from her phone, and embarrassing encounters.

"Juliet? Juliet? Wherefore art thou Juliet?"

With a grumble only she could hear, she shoved her phone into her back pocket.

"Those aren't the words."

Goosebumps glittered across her skin as anticipation rippled through her. She didn't want to see him, was convinced he didn't want to see her, and yet she was relieved to hear the thumping on the stairs that let her know he was on his way up to her.

"I do read, you know."

"Buzzfeed quizzes don't count as reading."

Goodness, she still had no idea where this snark was coming from, but she suspected it was because at the end of the day, she didn't really care what he thought of her. Not the way she wanted people in the Friends or at the library to like her. Working alongside Lucas was just something she had to do to help Denise. Then she never had to see him again. The town was big enough they'd likely never cross paths.

"How else am I supposed to know what houseplant I am?"

She bit the inside of her cheek, curiosity getting the better of her. "Which are you?"

"A chia pet."

She pressed her lips together to stop from smiling and gestured at the boxes in front of her. "You forgot this yesterday."

"Hey, I'm sorry for rushing off." Lucas ran a hand through his hair, his tone suddenly serious. "I didn't mean to leave you to finish up on your own."

Even if she was touched by the apology, she wasn't about to show it. "It's fine. You don't have to be here, you know. The Friends can take care of this."

His eyes darkened. "No, there are things here that belong with us."

"Then let's get to it." She picked up a book that had fallen out of a box. "The sooner we're done, the sooner we'll be out of each other's hair."

The afternoon started off slightly better than the previous day, since once he saw the number of bookshelves in the spare bedroom, he admitted that working in separate rooms would help speed things up.

It was much quieter this way, at least at first. Whenever she came across something that was unmistakably personal, like more photos, journals, or clippings from newspapers featuring the garden club, she'd carefully put those in their own box, having decided to wait until there was a big enough stack to go looking for him.

Lucas, however, didn't seem to feel the same. He barged into the bedroom with each and every single one of the items he wanted to make a case for the garden club keeping. Nearly everything he brought was clearly of value to him and couldn't be sold at a book sale, so of course, she agreed he could keep it.

Except when he was obviously trying to get away with something. Like the complete set of Austen's works in collectible hardcover that had never even been opened by the looks of the uncracked spines, despite his claims that they were her favorite books.

After the fifteenth interruption, she finally exploded—as she suspected had been his plan all along. "Can I please just have five minutes of peace?"

Her volume was borderline yelling and her tone was eight shades past irritated.

Instead of shouting back, Lucas's lips turned up at the corners. "I was wondering what you'd look like really upset."

Heat flooded her face. She inhaled deeply through her nose and let it out slowly through her mouth.

She couldn't get upset, couldn't let any inconvenient emotion get in the way of finishing this as soon as possible. "Well, now you've seen it, so please leave. We can pick this up again tomorrow."

"I work all day tomorrow."

Another deep breath before responding. "Then I'll do it myself. I've gotten the gist of what matters to you now. Don't worry, I'll put it all aside." She gestured to the box by her feet, which was now close to full of various books, journals, and knickknacks that anyone with half a heart could tell should be with someone who'd truly cared about Maude.

The half-smirk vanished from his face and his eyebrows drew together as he bent to look at the contents. He removed each paper carefully, looking at it like it was a lost treasure. "Where did you find all this?"

"All over." Taking a step back from where he hunched over the box, she rubbed her arms. The sudden softening of his mood after hours of irritation was unexpected. Everything about him was unexpected. The way she was feeling at the sight of his eyes growing misty with memories was the most unexpected—and the most unsettling.

"She wasn't that great about organizing. Everything was mixed in with her other books, or tucked at the end of shelves."

"That must have agitated you better than anything I did." He shot her a glance, a cocky eyebrow raised. The desire to stick her tongue out at him was nearly irresistible.

"What makes you say that? You don't know me." She put a hand on her hip. "My house could look like this. There could be chaos everywhere."

Standing, he crossed his arms and raised both eyebrows, his eyes now glittering with glee. "Is it now? I'd like to see that."

Her stomach flipped over. He couldn't possibly want to come over, to spend time with her outside of this project they'd been forced to collaborate on. He was just teasing, as usual.

"It can get chaotic when I'm focused on work. I just leave things wherever they land, until the project is finished."

"And then what do you do?"

A smile tugged at her pursed lips, as she tried and failed to suppress it. This victory could not be his. "I put things in their proper place, of course."

"Exactly." He shook his head, his hair grazing his ears. "I knew it."

She crossed her hands over her chest and narrowed her eyes. "How?"

"You're obviously an accountant or . . . " He tilted his head a little. "A Virgo sun sign."

"Ha! Wrong on both." She smiled smugly and leaned back against one of the now-empty bookshelves. "I'm an editor and a Capricorn."

"What's your rising?"

Flush and hang. "Virgo."

He grinned, showing all of his teeth, and she threw up her hands. "How do you even know about astrology?"

"I can't know anything about Shakespeare or astrology? Just plants?"

No.

She bit her lip to stop from saying it out loud. He was supposed to be just some guy she had to do this with, someone she would forget about when it was over. Not someone inter-esting or with anything in common with her.

Turning away from his piercing blue gaze, she inhaled deeply for the third time in as many minutes. There were countless people who read Shakespeare who knew their star chart. It didn't mean anything.

"I think that's enough for today." She looked down and nudged the box with her toe. "You should get this to your grandmother."

The calamondin orange tree was way too heavy for Lucas to carry on his own, but he didn't want to ask for Juliet's help. Especially since technically he didn't want her to see what he was doing.

Besides, she'd done enough already today to help him.

Saving the newspaper clipping about the club wasn't something he'd expected from her. Even knowing she was JCEdits, he'd never seen this side of her online. The careful way she'd put aside anything that even seemed remotely personal, arranging it all carefully into a box, like it was just as important to her as it was to him and his family.

His plan for the day had been to do the work quietly, be a considerate garden club member collaborating nicely with the Friends. Then, when Plantsguy95 talked more about the clubs, she'd have a good impression of them and want to help them.

His plan had not counted on the first words out of her mouth to be banter about Shakespeare and Buzzfeed quizzes. As all of his cousins could attest, it's not like he could just ignore something like that. Though Sage would have told him to try harder, to think of Granny.

He *had* thought about what was at stake. Briefly. But there was an irresistible pull to see her lips turn up in a smile. He got the impression she didn't spend much time laughing, and it was that much more rewarding to see it, to know he made her smile, since it was so hard won.

New plan: hopefully he'd irritated her enough that she'd complain to Plantsguy95 about it again and then he'd . . . well, he'd figure out what to do when it happened. He had six weeks to get her on the side of the garden club, and it was only day one.

"Looks like you could use some help."

With a sinking feeling in his belly, Lucas looked around the edge of the orange tree to see Heather standing next to his truck. He let the pot drop to the ground with a thud and hurried toward her.

"What are you doing here?" He took her by the arm and led her away from the house. "It's barely been twenty-four hours."

"I'm not here for that." She tugged her arm out of his grasp and walked toward the orange tree, holding out a Tupperware behind her. "Granny said you left this at her house this morning."

The cookies. Because of course Granny had made more.

He grabbed them from her hand and strode in front of her to block her path to the house. Before he could start scolding, however, Heather lit up and stuck her head out to peer behind Lucas's back. "Hi. I'm Heather, Lucas's cousin. You must be Juliet."

"Um, hi."

Confusion prickled along his neck. That didn't sound like the Juliet he'd spent the afternoon sparring with.

He turned to find Juliet was half in, half out of the house, eyes wide and bottom lip tucked under her teeth, as if unsure what to do and what to say.

Luckily, none of his cousins ever hesitated, so Heather waved and smiled without a second thought.

"Pretty random that Maude just, like, gave you her house, huh?"

In an instant, Juliet's hesitant demeanor disappeared. She

took a step forward on the porch and narrowed her eyes. "She gave it to the Friends of the Library, not me."

Heather let out a tinkle of a laugh. "Of course, that's what I meant."

"Why are you here?"

For the first time in his life, Lucas witnessed Heather flustered. She tucked a strand of hair behind her ears and glanced his way, but he just shook his head. *I'm totally not saving you from this*, he told her with his eyes.

"I was just passing by and saw Lucas's truck. I thought he might need some help."

"With what?"

"Nothing." Lucas grabbed Heather and positioned their bodies in front of the orange tree.

It was useless, of course. The thing was over six feet tall. Most kept indoors didn't reach that height, but Maude had taken exceptional care of them. Which was why he'd thought them important enough to sneak out of the house, away from the clueless Friends.

Now, the Geis women could glare. It was a family trait, passed down from mother to daughter, gaining strength with each generation. Heather's withering stare was the combined power of all her older cousins, and aunts, and mother, and Granny.

From her position on the porch, Juliet put her hand on her hips, and *glared*.

"Did you remove a plant from the house without discussing it with me?" Behind the frosty stare, she looked almost hurt. Like he'd just spit on all her work today to put aside the most precious of items in the house.

Pink crept across Heather's face and Lucas heard her swallow hard. She leaned in to whisper to him, "If she's this thorny with you all the time, then I like her."

Gathering his courage, and remembering that this was about Granny and the club, not the gorgeous glowering goddess in front of him he'd just pissed off, he made his way back up the stairs. "This is a very special one." He pointed back to the orange tree, where Heather was now checking the leaves for dust. "This was a gift from the club to Maude for her seventieth birthday."

Though her eyes softened a bit, Juliet stood firm, raising her chin and crossing her arms over her chest. "They should stay at the house until Denise can weigh in."

This close to her, almost nose to nose, she came exactly to his chin and her bright green eyes had flecks of gray in them. The back of his neck was prickly, like little rose thorns were sprouting at the base of it. "What does Denise want with them?"

Those gray-flecked green eyes held steady on his. "I don't know, but it's up to the Friends to decide, not you."

The *you* was laced with poison, and only Heather's quiet snickering behind him kept him from responding in kind. There was no doubt all the cousins would be getting a play-by-play within minutes of her leaving. More worrying, Granny would be hearing about this.

"How about we give her a call?" At Heather's suggestion, Lucas turned, his eyes wide and dangerous. Pulling her phone out of her back pocket, Heather looked almost ready to burst with glee at her suggestion. "And Granny, too."

"No." Lucas and Juliet spoke in unison.

"Too late, already dialed." She ran in the opposite direction down the driveway, too fast for them to follow.

"I thought your generation only texted," Lucas called after her, but she was already too far away to hear. He turned back to Juliet, ready to apologize—for the tree, for his cousin—but hesitated at the steely look on her face.

They were still close together on the porch. Too close, really. Close enough for her irritated exhale to coast across his cheek and send a zing of energy through his body. Close enough to see her pupils dilate and hear her next breath hitch in her throat. Close enough to notice a freckle right above her left eyebrow.

Every part of him wanted to step even closer, to eliminate the remaining distance between them.

Every part of him, except a tiny voice in his brain.

She doesn't know who you are.

With the strength it would have taken to lift two calamondin orange trees high above his head, he took a step back. Then another. Then he turned and made his way down the stairs.

"I'll put the tree back until we hear from Denise and Granny," he said without looking at her.

JCEDITS

I have a question and please don't take this the wrong way.

PLANTSGUY95

Uh oh, this sounds bad.

JCEDITS

I'm sorry, it was just a long, irritating day, and I need to know that not all plant people are like this.

PLANTSGUY95

Like what?

I'll need more details than that to provide an appropriate answer.

JCEDITS

Irritating, provoking, annoying, vexing.

PLANTSGUY95

Lol, I know I'm not the editor here, but those all sound like the same thing.

Is this still Mr. Darcy?

JCEDITS

Yes. And an interfering cousin, though not quite Mr. Collins' level of terrible.

PLANTSGUY95

I'm not going to Google that one, and just assume it's not a compliment.

So Darcy is a "plant person" is he? What does that mean?

JCEDITS

It means he's in the garden club.

PLANTSGUY95

Oh, so you did join. Great!

JCEDITS

No, I just have to work with them on something. I won't be joining now, that's for sure.

PLANTSGUY95

Ouch. Writing off a whole group just because of one jerk. I bet not everyone in the club is irritating.

Maybe he's just having a bad day.

JCEDITS

Maybe. Or he hates me for some reason.

PLANTSGUY95

I highly doubt that anyone could hate you.

JCEDITS

So he's just irritating by nature.

Not all garden club people, just him.

PLANTSGUY95

That sounds much more likely.

What are you working with them on? An editing project?

JCEDITS

I wish. It's complicated.

A territory issue, you might say.

PLANTSGUY95

Sharks and Jets?

JCEDITS

West Side Story you know, but not Pride and Prejudice? I told you there's a movie.

PLANTSGUY95

It's on my list, I promise.

Is the territory under dispute yours?

You realize I'm thinking this is like, bulletin board space at the supermarket, lol.

JCEDITS

Ha, no, more like a house.

PLANTSGUY95

Woah, fancy.

JCEDITS

They used it for a long time, but then the owner decided to give it to us.

I feel bad that they lost their space, but we didn't ask for it.

PLANTSGUY95

So what's your group planning on doing with it?

JCEDITS

No idea. For now, we're just cleaning it out. There are a ton of plants.

Is it ok if I send you a few pictures to get some maintenance tips? I want to be sure we take good care of them.

PLANTSGUY95

Do you really need to ask?

TEN

The day was hot for May, and Juliet was sweating through her t-shirt so badly she was tempted to go home and change. She might have, if she wasn't late for meeting her mother at the Greenhaven Community Fair. For once, her mom wasn't busy with her sister's family on a weekend, and had driven out to see her.

Knowing that Juliet wouldn't want to ride in the car with her, even the short drive into town center, her mom was meeting her there. Except they hadn't defined a meeting point, and her mom was a horrible texter, so now Juliet was wandering around, hot and grumpy.

Then she spotted the garden club's table, and she went from grumpy to pissed.

"GARDEN CLUB UPROOTED—HELP US PLANT THE SEEDS FOR A NEW PLACE TO GROW!"

Right across the lawn from their table was the one for the Friends of the Library, stacked high with books, bookmarks, and tote bags. There was no one perusing the selection, however. Stephen sat to one side in a folding chair, glaring darkly across the lawn where a crowd was bustling around Lucas holding court, speaking to everyone with that stupid charming smile plastered on his face and winking his brilliantly mesmerizing brown eyes.

The memory of standing mere inches from those eyes—and that mouth—sent a shiver through Juliet, despite the hot weather and her sticky shirt.

It had been four days since she'd last seen Lucas at the Periwinkle Mansion. He'd been unavailable due to work, and apparently no one else in the club was available to sift through Maude's things with Juliet. Though she had a sneaking suspicion he'd asked everyone to not be available, either to delay things even longer, or so he could be the one to annoy her.

Or both.

"Geis has gotten on your nerves, huh? That didn't take long."

Stephen was looking at Juliet now, and had apparently interpreted her shiver as an irritated one. Which, of course, it had been.

"It's true he's been a bit . . . pushy while cleaning out the house."

The fight over the orange trees had ended in a compromise between Denise and Mrs. Geis, who both had to come down to the house to look at the plants in question. Five would stay at the house, and Mrs. Geis would distribute the other five to the garden club members who wanted a reminder of Maude.

Remembering the reason she was the one to clean out the house instead of Stephen, Juliet hesitantly asked him, "How are you feeling?"

Stephen's eyes shifted away from her. "Fine, thanks."

Her spirits fell a bit, then hot embarrassment hit her for being disappointed. What had she expected, a fully detailed medical report? Even though he was sitting down, he was here, so clearly he was fine, just like he'd said.

"I can think of at least five slogans more creative than that," grumbled Stephen, waving at the garden club's sign.

Juliet's lips ticked up in a smile. It was comforting to know she was on the same side as someone, even if she was terrible at defending that side, and wished there didn't have to be sides at all.

The whole orange-tree dilemma shouldn't feel like a failure, but it did. Denise had asked her to help, but she'd just created more work by needing her to referee a ridiculous plant-distribution battle. These were the kinds of situations where Juliet felt the lack of experience of working in an office. When you worked for yourself, there was no negotiating with colleagues over projects or parking spaces. She'd never had to involve a third party to help her settle a dispute with someone else, or even have to settle one in person.

Everything was done on her own, online, where she could control and plan and think carefully. That should have been an advantage, but in this case, it had just pointed out how different Juliet was from everyone else, and how much Denise couldn't rely on Juliet to fight for the Friends.

Lucas was more than prepared to fight for the garden club, and he was winning by a landslide, all thanks to a terrible plant pun.

"A slogan doesn't need to be good to be effective." Pleased that Stephen was initiating conversation, Juliet kept going. "I assume if people go to his table first, they don't come over here?"

"Hmm."

Shifting on her feet, Juliet tried again. "Did most people really not know the club didn't own the house?"

"Why would they?" Stephen slid his eyes over to her and recrossed his arms. "It doesn't impact daily life here in the town at all. Who cares who owns it?"

"Lucas seems to really care." She realized what she said and felt the heat on her cheeks, but Stephen wasn't looking at her. He was still glaring over at the other table. "I mean, the garden club seems to care."

"No, you had it right. It's mostly Lucas. He's been like that his whole life."

Surprised, Juliet turned. "You know him?"

"I remember when he was in high school. I didn't teach him, but some kids you remember better than others. Especially when they organized a boycott of the football games when his cousin got dumped by the quarterback."

"That sounds intense." Also kind of sweet.

The sweetness must be long gone. With each person who passed by their table and turned away without even stopping to glance at a book, Juliet's pulse ticked up another notch. This was unfair. Whatever he was telling people was making them hate the library. Who hated libraries?

They did just as much for the community as the garden club. They supported after-school programs, and book boxes for kindergartners, and a lecture series. Not to mention the magazine that Juliet was going to help edit, once the work on the house was finally done. Which it would never be if Lucas kept putting it off.

Reaching into the cardboard box by Stephen's feet, Juliet found some string he must have used to hang the banner that was just their association name above the town logo. There were also extra membership sign-up sheets, blank on one side.

Two can play at this game.

"Do you mind if I use these?"

Stephen raised a curious eyebrow at her, then shrugged and returned his eyes across the lawn.

It took her almost ten minutes to fill in the block letters with a marker and thread the string through the papers, even though there was no one stopping by their table to interrupt her.

Stephen observed silently, his gaze occasionally flicking over to the garden club table, where people were still milling around.

"MAUDE   PERIWINKLE   SUPPORTED   THE FRIENDS—SO CAN YOU!"

When she finished hanging up the sign, her whole body trembled as she turned to see how Lucas would react. To see how everyone would react.

This went way beyond anything she'd ever done before, or even thought herself capable of. Now that it was done, looking up at her messy lettering, a shuddering wave of uncertainty whipped through her so fast, she almost fell over.

What on earth had possessed her to do this? This was just a group of people who wanted to fundraise for the library. This was not *West-Side-Story*-level drama.

The satisfaction at seeing Lucas's stormy expression, however, curled deep inside her chest in a way only a Leonard Bernstein song could capture.

In a dramatic moment fitting a stage show, just as Juliet was reaching for the chair to take the sign down, her mother appeared in front of her.

"There you are, dear. I've been looking everywhere for you."

"Mom." Juliet turned to Stephen, her stomach in a tight knot. He seemed unfazed, however, and nodded once in acknowledgment to the older woman.

"Is this the library organization you've been volunteering with?" Barely glancing at the sign above her head, she picked up a book and paged through it. "You spend a lot of time helping, it sounds like. They're lucky to have you."

"We are," Stephen said from his folding chair.

There was a lightness in Juliet's veins, propelling her upward. Her mom actually listened, and Stephen had given her an unexpected and kind compliment in just two words.

Her mom put the book back on the table. "When you said it

was a family event, I thought perhaps you were hinting at a boyfriend." She looked around before leaning toward Juliet to whisper in her ear. "Is there anyone you'd like me to meet?"

Just like that, she came crashing back down to earth.

"No, there's no one." Without consciously choosing to do so, her eyes flicked to the table across from hers to where Lucas was chatting with yet another person, like his sole mission in life was to get every last resident on his side.

Luckily, her mom didn't notice where Juliet's attention was. All she had eyes for was the lack of a significant other in her daughter's life. "Well, going to events like this should change that. Lots of nice young people here."

"Who are all here with their spouses and kids, Mom. This isn't where you meet someone when you're in your late thirties." If she even wanted to. Which, after the breakup, she most definitely didn't want to.

"I met your father at a pie-eating contest, so you never know."

"Pie-eating contest?" From behind the table, Stephen piped up. "That's how I met my husband."

A new wave of mortification rolled over Juliet as she was gently nudged aside so that her mom could chat with Stephen. The normally taciturn grumpus positively lit up as the two of them exchanged stories and pie recipes. Typical that even though she'd known and worked beside him for hours at the book sale, it took less than ten minutes for someone else to charm him into a conversation. Juliet was never anyone's first choice of conversation partner.

The hot day was finally too much, and Juliet knew she needed to get some hydration or risk truly falling over. Not wanting to interrupt the two new besties, she just gave a quick wave and mouthed "be right back" before wandering off in the direction of the snack tables and food trucks.

It wasn't a big deal, she knew that. Some people just clicked right away, and some people never warmed up to you. It was nothing personal—or rather, it was all personal, so there was no reason to go wishing you were somebody else. Except that's just what Juliet was doing as she reached into her pocket and pulled out a few wrinkled dollar bills.

Everyone knew Lucas. Even Stephen remembered him from years ago. Patrice at the library didn't even remember Juliet after meeting her multiple times.

Juliet inhaled and reminded herself this wasn't Lucas's fault. It wasn't his fault he had been in this town since he was born and had the support of everyone, while she'd just moved in a year ago and was a hermit who knew nobody.

As if summoned by her thoughts, she heard Lucas's voice right behind her.

"Your sign has a few inaccuracies we should talk about."

Juliet's fist tightened around the money, crumpling it even more. "So does yours." The smell of fried dough and beer wafted over to her from the food stands, and her stomach churned.

Instead of a snappy comeback, he laughed and fell into step beside her, like he belonged there, like they had made plans to meet up for a snack today.

"How does your mom know Stephen Liu?"

"She doesn't. They just met."

He ran a hand through his floppy hair. "They seem pretty friendly. Should your dad be worried?"

"My dad is dead."

"Oh."

Even before she saw the surprise and sadness in his eyes, she knew she'd been unnecessarily sharp.

"I'm sorry that was—"

"I'm sorry, I didn't—"

They both stopped and shared a small smile.

Lucas broke the awkward silence first and gestured at the closest food truck. "Can I get you an ice cream?"

"Is it because you feel bad that my dad died?"

"No," he said, a little too quickly. He shoved his hands into the pockets of his shorts. "It's because I have free coupons for working at the table and I don't want them to go to waste."

"Well, that's hard to argue with."

They stood slightly apart as they waited in the long, twisting line for ice cream, with Lucas several steps behind her. The air between them was heavier than normal. Every movement of his body made ripples that she felt on her skin. It was like the other day on the porch, but a hundred times worse because of the heat. She could almost taste the sweet saltiness of his sweat. When she inhaled deeply, the familiar dirt and moss smell lingered underneath.

Thankfully, the line was quicker than expected. A few awkward, wordless minutes later, they both had giant cones of soft serve and were making their way back to the rows of tables and booths of the fair.

It was her turn to break the awkward silence. "Thanks for the ice cream. Should your girlfriend or wife back there be worried?"

He frowned, lines appearing between his eyebrows. "You mean at the table? She's my cousin." A wide grin overtook his face. "I can't believe you thought Sage was my wife. I can't wait to tell her, she'll absolutely die—" His eyes went wide.

Juliet tried to hold back her laugh, but it burst out of her. "Really, it's fine. It was six years ago."

"That's pretty young to lose your dad."

She raised an eyebrow and her eyes flicked to the side. They were passing in front of the Senior Center's table. "How old do you think I am?"

He shook his head and held up a hand. "I have eight female cousins, counting Heather and Sage. I know better than to answer that question."

She laughed again.

"Any age is too young, I think."

His tone was oddly serious, and Juliet found herself wanting to dig deeper. There was something soft about him right now, almost vulnerable. He was leaving himself wide open for mocking, as if he wanted her to take a cheap shot in retaliation for whatever offense he thought he'd caused.

Instead, she changed the subject. "Eight cousins is a lot."

"Oh, that's just the women. I have five male cousins. And they all live here in Greenhaven."

A shudder ran through Juliet as she tried to imagine having that many family members nearby.

"I thought I had it bad with my mom two towns away."

"Bad?" He looked up from his ice cream, lips surrounded by chocolate. "It's amazing. My family is everything to me."

"Yeah, I figured. I just didn't realize you had such a big one."

Everything about him was family-oriented, garden club focused, and town-centric. It was the complete opposite of Juliet, and she found herself both jealous and confused.

"Is it just you and your mom?"

Juliet shook her head. "I have a sister who lives about an hour away. She's a lawyer at a big firm, and her husband runs triathlons. My mom takes care of their kids a few days per week, so I don't see her much."

"Except when she comes to bug you about having kids?"

She blushed and looked away into the crowd milling around them, full of parents with little ones riding on their shoulders or in strollers. Before responding, she took a bite of ice cream to cool down. "How did you know?"

"Um, hello, what do you think Granny asks me about every single day of my life since I turned thirty?"

"What do you tell her to get her to leave you alone?"

"That I'm not interested in kids right now, maybe ever. But if I ever am, I'd rather foster, like my parents did with me. They died in my twenties."

"Oh." Now it was her turn to shift awkwardly at the revelation of something so personal. Her stomach swirled. To have something so sad in common with Lucas was unexpected. Unsure what else to do, she spewed the first words that came to mind. "I'm, like, ninety-nine percent sure I don't want kids. In a few more years, it won't be possible anymore anyway, then my mom will leave me alone."

She felt her cheeks heat. Had she seriously just mentioned her biological clock to Lucas Geis? She'd also told him about her dad, which she almost never did. Instead of snark, today she seemed incapable of keeping any of her thoughts to herself when she was around him. It was horribly embarrassing but also oddly liberating.

Even though they hadn't known each other long, and he irritated her more than anyone she'd ever met, it was strangely easy to talk to him. Like some part of her recognized something familiar in him.

They were almost back at their respective tables, their ice creams eaten and their pace slowing. He turned to her with an odd look in his eyes, like he was preparing to beat her overshare by miles. Her chest tightened, squeezing her heart. Before he could say anything, however, someone cleared their throat, and they both turned to look behind them.

Denise and Mrs. Geis were both standing just a few feet away, and they did not look happy.

ELEVEN

Granny had three levels of glare, and this one was what the cousins referred to as the "Venus flytrap." It was deceptively gentle, meant to lure you into a false sense of security. Then once you'd spilled your guts—snap. It was too late to escape.

It was Denise who spoke first, however, her expression tight. "While I appreciate that both of you have . . . enthusiasm for these organizations, and the creative wordplay, the mayor isn't very happy."

Juliet had turned a bright pink and looked like she wanted to cry. This wasn't what he expected from her. She'd crafted her sign almost as soon as she'd arrived at the community fair. She'd stood up to Lucas about the orange trees the other day and never let him get away with anything at the house. Yet in front of Granny and Denise, she was positively quaking in her boots.

Then there was her online persona, so professional, and so funny in their messages. The paradox of who Juliet was had taken root deep inside of him, like a vicious weed that sprouted once, then was suddenly everywhere the next day.

It was why he'd gone after her earlier. She was endlessly fascinating, and he couldn't seem to stay away.

The scary thing was, he wasn't sure he wanted to stay away.

"Why's the mayor upset?" He lifted his chin, suddenly ready to defend Juliet's right to annoy the crap out of him. "If we have a sign, then the Friends should get a sign."

Granny pursed her lips, but one was twitching a little, so he knew she wasn't actually at Venus-flytrap-level mad . . . yet. "It's supposed to be a joyous event, something for the community. For families." She leaned into her cane and glanced over her shoulder at the garden club table. "I know you're upset about the house, Lucas, but please stop this campaign against the Friends."

"The sign says nothing about them." Lucas pointed in the direction of the table, and Sage, who was taking in this exchange with an *I told you so* smirk on her face. "We're raising money for a new location."

"So you've abandoned your plan to get back the house somehow?"

The lie was ready on his tongue, but he bit it back. It was impossible to lie to Granny, but that wasn't who he was worried about. He glanced at Juliet, her face framed by the booth behind her advertising one of the local legal firms. The twist in his gut had nothing to do with his family. He was already lying to her every second of every day. No need to add a layer.

"I do not see how that is relevant to the present situation."

"Lucas Edward Geis," Granny scolded, his knees turning to jelly at the tone. "You are a grown man, almost forty. You need to start thinking about someone other than yourself."

That hit him in the chest, hot and painful, as if she'd punched him. "I'm thinking about you, Granny. Maude was your best friend, and her house—"

"Has been gifted the way she intended."

"Are you saying you don't want the house back?"

"I'm saying the decision has been made, so there's no sense in trying to change it."

A steady stream of people browsing nearby tables wove around them. Denise and Juliet were following the conversation with their eyes, back and forth between the two Geises. It didn't really matter what Denise thought, but Lucas was surprised—and irritated—to find he cared a lot about what Juliet thought of him.

It was no secret from his behavior that he wasn't happy about cleaning out the house so the Friends could take it, but Granny had just made it clear he was actively looking for a way to get it back. Normally when he put a stake in the ground for a cause, he was laser focused on it, not worrying at all about the other side. This time it was different, and he hated it.

It felt too much like caring what a woman thought about him and his choices, and he'd sworn he'd never let that happen again.

"I didn't realize how personal this was for you, Lucas." Denise raised a hand to shield her eyes from the sun, the other hand coming to rest on Granny's arm. The two women glanced at each other. "Perhaps someone else in the garden club should finish up the work with Juliet at the house?"

"No!"

To his surprise, Juliet had voiced her disagreement at the same time as him. Turning to her, she flushed under his surprised gaze. Though it could have been the heat. The flowy shirt she was wearing clung to her skin, and a few strands of hair had escaped her ponytail, framing her bright-green eyes. There was something determined in them that got his heart pounding.

"It's just . . . " She hesitated and looked between the two older women. "We have a system, and we're almost done."

He raised an eyebrow. The "system" was Lucas pestering her, and they still had five rooms to go through.

Fluttery, swirly stirrings suddenly appeared in his belly.

Probably the ice cream. Dairy had not been his friend since his early thirties.

Denise and Granny both looked at Juliet, then at each other. There was a tiny tilt of Granny's lips, and a small arch to Denise's eyebrows that Lucas did not appreciate, but he wasn't about to contradict Juliet. He wanted to keep looking around the house for Maude's letters or journals.

From down the row of tables and booths, Sage caught Lucas's eye and waved him over, the crowd in front of the table still swarming with people. Maybe he couldn't change anything, but not knowing if Maude really wanted this was eating at him. His cousins would say it was because he was an insufferable know-it-all, but that wasn't it. When things didn't make sense— when people didn't make sense—it made him want to dig deeper, figure it out.

He couldn't figure out why Maude had made her choice, and he couldn't figure out Juliet. A few more weeks working together at the house, plus a little gentle nudging from Plants-guy95, and his plan would be finalized. Next steps would be clear and actions could be taken to get back what he—and the club—cared about.

Granny leaned heavily enough on her cane that it sank an inch into the grass. "Are you sure you want to keep working together?"

Juliet and Lucas both nodded.

Denise sighed and looked at Granny, who nodded. "Well then, please try to finish up by Tuesday. The Friends need to start moving in their stock so the library can get their storage room back."

Lucas's stomach flipped over. That was in three days. Not nearly enough time to find anything significant, either from Maude or Juliet.

The shortened time frame didn't phase Juliet, who smiled. "No problem."

"I should have the final files for you to edit by then, as well," Denise said.

Lucas didn't know what Denise was talking about, but Juliet's smile widened and her eyes lit up. Without glancing his way again, she told both women she had to go find her mother, and headed off toward the Friends' table. She didn't glance back at him, but her head did turn toward the garden club's table, where Sage was still overwhelmed with the crowd. While he knew he should go help his cousin, Lucas just stood there, wondering what on earth had just happened with Juliet.

There was only one way he could figure it out.

PLANTSGUY95

How was the community fair?

JCEDITS

Surprisingly good, actually.

PLANTSGUY95

No books were thrown?

No plants were damaged?

JCEDITS

We behaved ourselves, despite some aggressive sign wars.

Though my mom was there.

PLANTSGUY95

That's a bad thing?

JCEDITS

She was only there to see if I had a secret boyfriend.

That's all she cares about. Not about the work I do, either volunteer or paid.

PLANTSGUY95

I'm sorry. That must be disappointing.

JCEDITS

It is, but I'm used to it by now.

Though I'm hoping winning this editing award may change things, or at least be something she can understand.

PLANTSGUY95

Editing award?

JCEDITS

It's not, like, a huge deal or anything.

It's just hard when I don't have a traditional promotion or fancy job title for her to brag about, like she can with my sister.

This will give her bragging rights.

PLANTSGUY95

Aren't you the one who should be bragging?

JCEDITS

I haven't won anything yet.

PLANTSGUY95

You'll win it for sure.

JCEDITS

That is impossible for you to know, and you have zero professional qualifications that would make your judgment of my skills relevant.

. . . but thank you.

TWELVE

Walking home from the grocery store the next night, the full bags in her hands bumping against her legs, Juliet was still thinking about the conversation with her mother at the fair after she'd left Lucas with Denise and Mrs. Geis. There'd been the expected grilling over who the "attractive, suave man" was—who used the word "suave" anymore? Answer: her mother—but there'd also been something else. An offhand comment as her mom was leaving, just a few words, but the gist had been something like, "I'm so glad to see you settled and truly a part of this town."

Had she really seemed like a part of everything? The silent houses on both sides of the street she was walking down were as unfamiliar as ever and had no answers for her.

Belonging somewhere was what she'd always wanted, and yet that's not how it had felt yesterday. It had felt like she was even more on the outside than ever.

In addition to the garden club, Lucas had a staggering *thirteen* cousins. Denise and Mrs. Geis clearly interacted on a regular basis as community nonprofit leaders. Even Stephen had old colleagues from the high school who had stopped by to see him at the table. Everyone other than her had connections. The one time she tried to stand up for an organization she was starting to truly feel a part of, she'd managed to antagonize the mayor. The silent houses around her now seemed to be wide-eyed and horrified with her.

This was why she basked in the simplicity of her online friendships. They were so easy, so effortless. Plantsguy95 was so supportive with so few words.

There was a ripping sound, and Juliet stumbled over the produce that was tumbling out of the paper bag in her right hand that was now in shreds.

A few choice curse words slipped out under her breath.

"Need some help?"

A trickle of hope flowed into her veins until she recognized the voice behind her.

"I'm fine." Irritation roiled in her stomach, and she bent down to drop her other grocery bag and collect what had fallen. Everything was slowly rolling away from her, thwarting her attempts to gather the fruit.

One particularly big orange rolled to a stop right at Lucas's feet. When he stooped to pick it up, she caught his eye, and realized he was in running shorts and a short-sleeved top. A slight sheen of sweat coated his arms that were thickly corded with muscle and on full display. His tattoos were even more visible.

Heat rushed to her face. Thankfully, it was early evening and in the slowly dimming light, whatever blush had decided to make an appearance shouldn't have been too obvious.

"Are you sure you don't need help?"

"Fine."

There was no good reason to not let him help her, other than the lingering embarrassment of everything she'd told him yesterday. The words that flowed so easily with him might reveal something she wasn't ready to share. This lingering need to connect with someone, anyone, was safer to direct to the Friends as a group, not any one individual.

Juliet suspected that's why Maude had left the house to a group, rather than one person. Though, the language around community use she'd included in the will was vague. Did she mean the library community or the larger Greenhaven community? Juliet briefly wondered if she should offer her editing services to lawyers, but that would mean asking her sister for advice and referrals. No thank you.

"You seem lost in thought."

Picking up the unbroken bags, she shook her head. "Just thinking about why Maude left the house to the Friends."

"Isn't that the million-dollar question." He sighed and stood up as well, his arms full of fruit. "I don't mean to be so stubborn about things. Change isn't easy for me."

"Me neither." The words were out of her mouth before she could stop them, the surprise that they had something in common loosening her lips. Though at this point, she shouldn't really be that surprised.

A smile spread across his face, like he was thinking the same thing. "No kidding. I'd never have guessed that about you."

There was a flutter in her chest at how well he already seemed to know her.

"So where's your car?"

"I don't have one."

"You don't have a car?" The shock in his voice was a familiar one for Juliet, and just like that, she was reminded how very unlike most people she truly was.

Rather than explain, she swallowed hard and shook her head.

"No. I don't need one when everything is so close."

"Until you buy eight pounds of oranges. Your arms must be

made of steel. What on earth do you need so much citrus fruit for?"

Instead of asking more about her car-less life, he'd let it drop. Her shoulders relaxed and her mouth turned up into a smile. "Avoiding scurvy."

He snort-laughed. "How very piratical of you."

Despite some lingering quaking in her stomach, Juliet chuckled. "I'm not that much further. Just another block. If you can manage?"

"Like I'd really admit it if I couldn't. Heather still won't let me forget I needed her to help me get the orange trees in the truck the other day."

"I won't tell her, promise."

With his arms full of fruit and a bag of green peppers looped around his wrist, he started walking beside Juliet. Even under the sharp citrus smell, there was Lucas, all fresh soil and summer rain.

"Oh, that's not a promise anyone can keep. Not around my cousins."

"There's literally no way I'd ever have any interaction with them unless they came to a book sale."

"You never know. This is a pretty small town. Lots of quilting circles and such."

"No, I grew up in a small town. This . . . " She looked around at the tree-lined street. "This town is the right size for me. Small enough I can walk to the town center, but big enough I don't see the same people all the time." See the same people, be judged by them. That was the worst part of a small town. Everyone knew everyone's business.

It had been less than two days at her mother's house after the breakup that people had started to stop her in the street to discuss The Ex. The gesture was sweet, but all she'd wanted was to never talk about it again. Then when she'd stopped talking, they'd all filled in the gaps.

"You manage to run into me quite a lot."

She'd been thinking the same thing, but hadn't wanted to point it out.

"Well, that's on you. What were you doing in this area?"

"I was at my cousin Mari's house helping her repot some plants."

"I'm sorry, now you'll need to walk all the way to your car—"

"It's a nice night. I ran there and was going to run back."

They walked in silence for a few minutes. It wasn't an uncomfortable silence, but vibrations in the air seemed to stretch from his skin to hers as their steps and pace synchronized.

He cleared his throat. "Thank you, by the way."

"For what?" She glanced at him, but he was facing forward, his eyes on the sidewalk in front of them.

"For arguing to let me keep helping at Maude's house. You didn't have to do that."

No, she didn't. And she still had no idea why she had.

Rather than ponder that, her mind focused on the practical consequences of her spontaneous support of his continued help at the house. Like making sure they finished up by Tuesday so Denise would get her the magazine she was supposed to edit. The BOC deadline was fast approaching, and she had to submit a completed, invoiced project.

"What time can you be at the house tomorrow?"

"I have to take Granny to a doctor's appointment, but it should be done by ten."

"Can you stay all day? We still have a lot of rooms to go through."

"I'll stay as long as it takes."

They'd reached her apartment building.

"This is me."

He nodded, opened his mouth, then closed it again.

She sighed. "Let me guess, you know someone else who lives here?"

"No, I just remember when it was built. This used to be an empty lot when I was in high school. We'd skip school and skateboard."

"Skip school?"

He chuckled.

"Probably not something you ever did. I bet you were all about the AP classes."

The air was thick with the smell of the oranges in his arms. A little tremble went through her spine. He already knew her so well, and they'd only just met.

Blinking like she'd been staring into the sun, she cleared her throat. "Thank you for stopping to help me."

"That's what neighbors do."

THIRTEEN

Lunch with Mari was usually a very relaxing event. They did it once every few weeks, whenever their schedules lined up between him at the hardware store and her at the dental office. The Chips and Chops Sandwich Shop was in between their respective workplaces, right in the center of town.

Except today, he wasn't meeting her on a break from work,

but on a much-needed escape from Maude's house. It was day two of the rush to get everything done by the random deadline Denise had set. Thanks to her messages to Plantsguy95, Lucas figured the files Denise had mentioned the other day must be for the editing award Juliet was entering. Without a cleaned-up house, Juliet wouldn't even get the chance to submit to the award.

This was not the kind of inside information he'd been thinking he'd get when he had come up with step three in his plan to get the house back. Instead of continuing with step four —dragging things out at the house as long as possible—now he breezed through stacks of books and papers, glancing only for a moment rather than examining every page carefully. Getting done quickly so Juliet could get what she wanted was important too. After all, this had never been about making things hard for her personally.

He hadn't given up on finding what he was looking for, of course. He never would. This was just a slight delay. Everything from Maude's more personal papers was all going to the garden club, stored at Granny's house, so Lucas could take his time looking through them later. Granny would be able to guide him, since she might know where in the journals would be the most likely place.

Except Granny wasn't exactly happy with him at the moment. Lucas was hoping Mari could help him with that.

Lucas walked into the sandwich shop and waved at the owner, Susan, who he'd known since high school. Without stopping at the counter, she knew what to make him. Sometimes it was nice to have someone know you so well.

And sometimes it was the worst. He caught his cousin's gleaming eye, and could tell she was going to want to talk about Granny and Maude's house. And Juliet.

"A little birdie told me you walked your new Friend home

the other night." The way she leaned on the word *Friend* let him know it was capitalized.

"What birdie?"

"Angela Relish. She lives in Juliet's building."

Of course she did. Between the thirteen cousins, Lucas had less than two degrees of separation from everyone in town. It didn't usually bother him, but today it did.

He ran a hand across his face and groaned. "People need to mind their own business." Except for him, of course. "How's that new boyfriend of yours doing?"

Mari chuckled and sipped her iced tea. "Nope, you had your chance at family dinner last week to get those details. Today is all about you." With the way her eyes shone, however, and the way she'd been looking at the guy all through dinner, Lucas knew things were going well. It filled him with warmth to see Mari so happy, even as she tortured him.

"Has the wind gone out of your battleship to get Maude's house back?"

He shot her a look. "Not even a little."

"Granny wants you to chill out."

"I'm doing this for her."

Mari didn't respond, but her pursed lips and raised eyebrow let him know exactly what she was thinking.

Lucas buried his head in his hands to avoid looking at her judgy face.

Why was everyone so convinced he had selfish motives for this? It was like no one else cared that a vulnerable old woman might have been tricked out of doing what she really wanted with her own house. No one else cared that over fifty years of town history was being erased in a matter of days, packed away into boxes. The garden club had raised more than enough money to rent a new space, but it would be in one of the bland meeting rooms in a random town building. There'd be no roots, and yes he knew that was a terrible pun, but he couldn't be the only one who was unhappy about it.

After a few silent moments glaring at his cousin, Susan brought over their food.

"How's it coming with Plantsguy95?" Mari asked.

"Shh, don't say it so loud." He glanced around the small sandwich shop. The line to order was almost out the door and the few tiny tables inside were all full of people grabbing a quick bite like they were. "You know I don't want anyone in town knowing about my account."

Mari rolled her eyes, but didn't comment. She knew why the topic stressed him out, had been there through the worst of the breakup.

Lowering her voice, Mari leaned closer. "Have you got you-know-who on your side yet or gotten any inside info on the Friends?"

Lucas grumbled around a mouth full of turkey club. "It's not really going as planned."

Juliet didn't know anything about Denise's plans for the house, and she wasn't going to suddenly switch allegiance to support the club, if the last few days at the house were any indication. While she was still putting aside anything that could be of sentimental value, they'd spoken less than a dozen words to each other.

The only "inside info" he'd gotten was about Juliet herself, and knowing more about her was doing weird things to his digestive tract. It was like they'd both gotten embarrassed by how much they'd told each other about their lives. Now they were treating each other like strangers, the house sucking all the conversation out of them. Every bookshelf they cleared and box they filled was one less hour that he had to plead his case for the garden club.

It wasn't much better in his messages to JCEdits. She was

clearly distracted or upset. Or maybe he'd imagined those hints of online flirting. After all, she didn't know who he was, so he probably only occupied that space in your brain where you didn't think about someone unless they were directly in front of you.

"I'm sure you'll think of something." Mari gave him a smile, her teeth perfectly white and even thanks to her employee discount with Dentist Danielle. "You always do."

The bell above the door jingled as someone new walked in. There was a shift in the air, and even before Mari's eyes lit up like Christmas morning, Lucas knew that Juliet had walked into the sandwich shop.

They'd both left Maude's house at noon, and agreed to meet back there at two to finish up the last room. Lucas assumed she'd gone home to eat, and he hadn't told her where he was going. That would have been against the new, unspoken, "no more than four words at a time to each other" rule that had been in place the last two days.

It was a small shop. There would be no avoiding her. But he didn't have to draw attention to himself and Mari. Juliet had already been subjected to Heather, seemed terrified of Sage, and he didn't want Mari to stick her nose any further into his business than it already was. Even if she was technically on his side.

Of course, that's not how his family worked.

All it took was a little nod of acknowledgment from Lucas, and Mari was nudging him out of the way to look her straight in the eye.

"Hello. I'm Mari."

Juliet approached their side of the counter slowly, biting her lip with one eye on the large menu above them. "Hi. Let me guess, one of Lucas's cousins?"

"Oh, has he mentioned me?" Mari preened a bit. "I assume he said I was his favorite cousin."

Juliet chuckled, an instant smile on her face. It was Mari's way. Like the flowers they were named after, all of his cousins had their individual charms. Heather was a budding thorny rose, Sage was a bristly cactus all squishy once you got past her spikes, but Mari was warm and golden like the sun.

"Is he allowed to have a favorite?"

"Well, not officially, but he knows what's best for him."

"Um, hello, I'm sitting right here."

"Eat your sandwich, Lucas, the grownups are talking."

"I'm older than you," he mumbled and shot Mari an evil look.

Still, he did as he was told, and kept eating, reassured that their small talk was a good thing. Juliet didn't know many people in town, outside of the Friends. Even if she didn't want the small town experience, it was always nice to know a few friendly faces.

Except that didn't explain why their easy interaction was filling his chest with a pleasant, happy glow. It shouldn't matter that his cousins all seemed to like her. It wasn't like *he* liked her or anything.

Well, he didn't dislike her, obviously. The only reason her recent cooling off was bothering him was because it was another obstacle to overcome in his quest to restore Maude's house to its rightful occupants.

"We get started around seven-thirty but the show doesn't start until eight."

With a jerk of his head so quick that he heard his neck pop, Lucas pulled himself out of his wandering thoughts to stare at Mari. "I'm sorry, what?"

"I wasn't talking to you Lucas." She rolled her eyes. "I was just telling Juliet when to arrive for *Bachelor* night at Sage's house."

"Why?"

A quick glance at Juliet's slightly pink face sent his heart racing. Had his cousin just forced her into something she didn't want to do? Mari's warmth was usually put to good use, like calming down stressed dental patients, but it could also be used for evil. Like ruining Lucas's life.

"Because I've never seen it, and Mari makes it sound like a lot of fun." Despite the flush of her cheeks, there was a defiant tilt to her chin that dared him to tell her not to go. "I don't have anything to do tonight, and she was nice enough to invite me."

"Are you sure?" Just thinking about her surrounded by his melodramatic, reality TV worthy family made his belly do somersaults inside his abdomen.

It was a terrible idea. They'd eat her alive.

Or worse, she'd reject them, mock them, the way his ex had. Lucas knew better now, wouldn't let some outsider interfere with his relationship with his family. A fierce wave of protectiveness rushed over him, and he narrowed his eyes at her. She frowned, biting her lip in a surprised confusion at his glare

No, Juliet wasn't the type to speak badly of others—other than him, of course, and he usually deserved it. His cousins would love that about her, take her under their collective wings and she'd become a more permanent fixture in the large, extended Geis social web.

Why did that thought both terrify and excite him?

Taking a bite of his sandwich, he used the chewing time to smooth out his expression before speaking. "It's just not exactly a quilting circle."

"I think I can handle watching an hour of television with some new f-friends." The slight stutter on the last word pinched at Lucas's heart.

He was being ridiculous. If she was a friend of her cousins, that didn't mean she had to be in his life.

"I'm sure you'll have a great time." Lucas turned to Mari and narrowed his eyes. "As long as everyone *behaves* themselves and doesn't talk about anything . . . unrelated to *The Bachelor*."

Mari batted her eyelashes at him, the picture of innocence.

"Why, whatever else would we talk about, dear cousin of mine?"

Lucas shook his head and sighed. *This was a terrible idea.*

FOURTEEN

This was a terrible idea.

With a wineglass in one hand, and a bowl of popcorn wedged between her knees, Juliet was seriously considering faking a stomach bug to go home. *Bachelor* night with the Geis cousins was going well, but it was only a matter of time before she did or said something to ruin everything like she always did.

When they asked her directly what she thought about something, she answered and they listened, then they moved on to the next person. No pressure to have the most insightful comment or know everything that was going on, which was nice. When the third commercial break rolled around, she'd been feeling comfortable enough to attempt a joke, and they'd all burst into laughter.

It was now the final commercial break before the rose ceremony, and there were squeals and shushing as more wine was poured and final snacks were grabbed from the kitchen. The excitement was palpable and Juliet couldn't help getting swept up in it. She didn't really care what was happening in the show, but she liked how all of these women cared so much about it, and each other.

Despite being the youngest, Heather had some of the most insightful comments on the emotional state of the contestants.

Sage, the hostess, making sure everyone had drinks and followed the no talking rule.

Mari, who'd stayed by her side all evening, like Charlotte had at the editor's conference. Her emotional support extrovert.

Lily and Ivy were twins who both had twins and seemed thrilled to talk about something besides nap times and feeding schedules.

Jasmine and Dahlia co-owned a hair salon in town and had the most hilarious comments on the hairstyles of all the contestants, but mostly on the bachelor himself.

And Violet, who'd said even less than Juliet all night, would occasionally catch her eye and give a small shrug-smile combo that seemed to say, *Yeah, I know they're a lot, but they're great, I promise.*

Obviously, Juliet had to leave now, while they all still liked her. She had made one successful joke and was enjoying herself, but it was almost too good to be true. There was no way they'd actually accepted her so quickly. They were being polite, perhaps even including her to irritate Lucas, both of which were fine with her.

A perfectly highlighted blonde was talking to the camera with wide, tear-filled eyes, explaining how all over the place her emotions were about staying on the show.

Juliet could empathize. The last few days at Maude's house had been . . . confusing, to say the least. She and Lucas had barely spoken. It was as if all the things they'd said to each other at the fair and when he'd walked her home were floating around the house, hiding in the various plants.

Maybe it was just a weird guy thing, but she had no way of knowing. The only guy she knew relatively well at this point was Plantsguy95, and she wasn't about to ask him for advice. Especially when her feelings for him were just as complicated as they were for Lucas. So rather than talk or text with either of them, she did what she did best: she kept quiet and observed.

"Juliet." Mari leaned over and touched her arm. "Where'd you go? You looked miles away."

"Still thinking about what Shannon said to Krista?" Heather shook her head. "There's no way she's staying now."

Juliet chuckled and returned her focus to the TV.

You can't leave before the end of the show, she told herself. There were only a few minutes left. In order to be ready to go as soon as it was over, she started inching her way down the couch. Standing and putting her hands over her head—careful not to spill the wine—she stretched and grabbed the bowl of popcorn.

"Just need a refill before the big finale."

Alone in the kitchen, she reached for her phone, thinking she'd send an update to Charlotte, who'd helped her prepare for tonight with suggestions on what to wear and what not to say. Her heart gave a little stutter when there was a message from Plantsguy95 waiting, the first in a few days. Hesitating only for a moment, she opened it up, and a smile spread across her face.

PLANTSGUY95

Work has been crazy busy for me too this week.

I was thinking about your garden club Darcy and I have a theory.

JCEDITS

So you finally read the book?

PLANTSGUY95

Of course not.

Do you want to hear my theory or not?

JCEDITS

Actually, not that much interaction with him lately.

I can confirm, however, that it's definitely just Darcy who's vexing, not the whole club.

PLANTSGUY95

We'll return to your outdated use of "vexing" later.

Spending some time with the garden club after all then?

JCEDITS

Sort of. This isn't technically a garden club event, but I think they're all involved in a way.

PLANTSGUY95

Maybe there's a way for your group to work with them?

JCEDITS

If it were up to me, sure. But it's not.

PLANTSGUY95

Sounds like you do a lot for your group. You sure your opinion won't matter?

JCEDITS

My opinion never matters.

PLANTSGUY95

I bet it does when it really counts.

Her chest tightened. *Like when I insisted only Lucas could finish cleaning out the house with me and they actually listened.*

"Juliet, you're going to miss it," someone called from the living room.

Dahlia popped her head into the kitchen. "Just wait until you see what dress they put her in."

"Lily took your spot on the couch, so you'll either have to shove her off or sit on her."

Warmth spread through Juliet's body, blocking out the nervous whisper in her mind that they didn't really want her here. Taking a deep breath, she refilled her popcorn bowl and headed back.

Sitting on Lily was not an option, so Juliet tucked herself next to the arm of the couch and leaned her head against it. Violet caught her eye again and gave her a smile. Mari looked around and gave her a thumbs up when she spotted her. Sage shushed everyone as the intro music played, letting them know the commercial break was over.

In a few minutes, it was all over. A sobbing girl had left empty handed, and another was beaming at the camera, rose in hand. While the others erupted into their thoughts, Juliet was overwhelmed by shame and embarrassment on behalf of the girl not chosen. The popcorn in her mouth was dry, and a large gulp of wine did nothing to ease the aching of her throat as tears pricked at her eyes.

How awful, to be put on the spot like that. The familiar string of Juliet's heartbreak being discussed nonstop by everyone in her hometown made its way into her chest.

This, however, was public humiliation to an extreme level. At least some of the Geis women seemed upset about the final choice, but none of them seemed to care about the rejected contestant's feelings.

"What happens to her now?" Juliet heard herself asking, though she wasn't sure anyone heard her over the sounds of nine adult women all speaking at once.

Lily, who was closest to her, stopped her conversation with Ivy mid-sentence to answer Juliet. "Oh, she probably already has a few media contracts lined up. She was popular enough that she might come back as the *Bachelorette*. Or she'll go home, back to her job, the way a lot of them do."

"Oh." Juliet let that sink in. "So she'll be fine? Even though her heart was just broken on national TV?"

Lily frowned. "I don't know that it's real heartbreak."

Mari let out an exaggerated gasp. "You mean reality TV isn't real?"

Everyone else laughed, and Juliet shifted in her position next to the couch, aware of a few more eyes on her than before.

"I mean, the emotions are real." Heather leaned across the coffee table to steal a chip from Mari's bowl. "But being isolated for weeks with nothing to watch or read heightens things to a way different level than you get in real life. Add in all those cameras, knowing people are watching you, it must get really intense."

"Isolation equals more emotions for sure," Mari said. "I met my boyfriend when we got stuck in an elevator together. That was only a few hours, not weeks, but it turned every thought and feeling up to an eleven out of ten."

Everyone besides Juliet gave a little wistful sigh. The story must have been a good one.

"Besides, it's week five," Heather said. "I don't think this is, like, *heartbreak*, heartbreak. Not season finale level, anyway."

The others nodded.

"You'll keep watching with us until then, won't you, Juliet?" Mari smiled at her from across the room, sandwiched between Violet and Dahlia on the couch angled to the TV. "Five more shows to go until the finale."

The potential for heartbreak was unquestionably there. They wanted her now, but that could change in an instant. The cool burst of air-conditioning from the vent above hit her neck, and she suppressed a shiver. The room was warm. These women were warm. Life was less dramatic than reality TV, but there were certain moments in Juliet's life that, at least in her memory, were just as dramatic.

However, with everyone's eyes on her, what else could she say but yes?

FIFTEEN

JCEDITS

I have a deadline coming up and I feel like I might fall into one of my intense work sprints.

I don't want Pete to die again.

PLANTSGUY95

He didn't die last time. You got him healthy again.

JCEDITS

I would prefer to not have it take weeks and weeks. What should I do?

PLANTSGUY95

I recommend taking breaks from work to feed yourself and your plants.

JCEDITS

Stop, you sound like my mom.

PLANTSGUY95

Just what every guy likes to hear.

JCEDITS

What about the wine bottle filled with water trick?

Didn't you post about that for people who go on vacation?

PLANTSGUY95

Sure, that could help it from completely drying out.

Make sure the soil is fully moist beforehand.

Maybe leave it in a sink where it can drain.

Too much water is just as bad as too little.

JCEDITS

You're the best.

PLANTSGUY95

Now that's what every guy likes to hear.

Pride and Prejudice was undoubtedly the most boring book Lucas had ever read.

He had no logical reason for why he was sitting in the courtyard at Cork and Beans Café with a too-sugary iced coffee and the book open before him, other than what his cousins called his congenital stubbornness. The decision had been made to read it, so he was reading it. Even if it was taking weeks because he started to doze off every other paragraph. Even if there was no way he'd be able to use any of this to help Plantsguy95 convince Juliet or JCEdits to support the garden club getting back the house.

It was growing harder and harder in their interactions online to remember his goal. Their last exchange had only been about plants, and yet he'd been way more flirty than he usually was. She hadn't responded to his last message, and he worried it had been too obvious, too much. If she stopped talking to him completely, that wouldn't help anything.

He took a sip of his iced drink and gritted his teeth at the sweetness. They had finished up at Maude's house the previous week, so there was no more guaranteed daily interaction. Maybe he'd run into her around town, but if she was about to go into another intense work period, there was no way to know when that would be over. All he had now was their online messages, and she'd already brushed him off once before. At least this time she was giving him a heads up, which felt like progress.

What he really wanted to know was how *Bachelor* night had gone, but of course he couldn't ask JC about that online. None of his cousins were giving him details, other than "she's really nice and funny." He already knew that. What he didn't know was what to do next.

Which is why he was reading about Mr. Darcy. Maybe it would inspire something useful, like a scene or phrase that would unlock everything with her. The ice rattled in his cup when he took another sip of coffee. He'd only gotten it because of how hot it was today, and he regretted it even more than he did the decision to read this book.

The only part that stuck out was a line about losing the good opinion of someone forever. He wasn't sure he'd ever be able to overcome Juliet's first horrible impression of him, and his cousins seemed intent on making things worse at every opportunity. Just like they had with his ex, Audrey.

No, that wasn't fair. That had all been his own failure, not theirs.

Now he was failing at this too. He should just move on to some other plan that had nothing to do with Juliet. There were still stacks of Maude's boxes at Granny's to go through. There was a new location to look for. There was the fall programming and planting schedule to prepare for the next meeting. How

Juliet felt about him wouldn't make any difference in any of that.

Squinting in the sunlight, he stretched in his chair and looked around at the mostly empty courtyard of the café. Getting Juliet to like him was not the goal. Even if she was funny and sweet, she was intense and sharp and confusing.

Just as he picked up his book to start his third attempt to finish chapter fifteen, Juliet appeared in the doorway that led from the main part of the café into the courtyard.

There was a pinch in his chest that was the most confusing of all. At least, until her face seemed to light up for a split second at the sight of him before settling into a frown.

Now *that* was confusing.

With only the smallest of hesitations, she stomped over to him. A messenger bag was hanging heavily on her shoulder. She held a notebook in one arm and gripped a steaming cup of something in the other hand.

"You're at my table."

In an attempt to get his heart and head to pick a side and stick to it, he leaned back in his chair and took a long sip from his drink. He gritted his teeth again. "Hello to you too."

"I work at this table every Wednesday from one to four."

Lucas glanced at the time on his phone. It was twelve fifty-seven. "I don't see a reserved sign on it."

Her cheeks flushed, and her eyes sparkled, and Lucas wanted to jump out of his seat and run in the other direction because of what that did to his belly. "It's not my table in that way. Just that I always work here."

"What happens when it rains?"

"I stay at home."

"So you could go home and work."

"It's not raining, and I'm already here."

"Well, the table is plenty big for the two of us. Happy to share."

She bit her lip, and he could tell she was considering arguing some more. Then the clock in the town hall struck one, and the bell started ringing. The need to stick to her timetable must have won out over whatever ambivalence or distaste she felt for him. She sat in the chair opposite him, pulled out a laptop from her bag and plugged it into the power strip under the table with the practiced air of someone who'd been working at this table from one to four every Wednesday for months.

"Just please don't talk, okay?"

"No wonder they liked you at *Bachelor* night."

She pursed her lips and narrowed her eyes.

He chuckled and gestured to the book in front of him. "I've got my own stuff to do."

Slipping in two wireless earphones, she nodded once, then went into a super-focused stare at her screen. The only things that moved were her eyes and a single finger on the trackpad as she scrolled. Occasionally, she'd jot something down in her notebook.

It should have been boring. After all, all he could see was Juliet, quiet and concentrated, barely moving and not talking.

And yet Lucas was riveted.

He always wondered how JCEdits could ignore eating, sleeping, and showering, but he had the proof right before him. She had the look of someone completely absorbed in their work in a way he'd never felt about the dozens of different jobs around town. It was how his ex had wanted him to be about his social media.

With a sudden intake of breath, she turned her head and looked away, her eyes coming to rest on Lucas, who quickly returned his gaze to the open book in his hand.

"What are you reading?"

"Hmm?" He dragged his eyes from the page where he'd absolutely not taken in a single word, met her curious gaze, then flicked back to the book. "Oh nothing really. *Pride and Prejudice.*"

A beat passed. "You just decided to read it randomly on a Wednesday?"

"First Shakespeare, now Austen. I would love to know why you think I don't read."

"I would love to know why you never answer my questions."

"Fine, I'll answer one for every question you answer for me."

She raised an eyebrow and took a sip of her drink. "Can I pick dare instead?"

A burst of laughter pushed out of him, and the corners of her lips curled up above the edge of her cup.

"Fine," she said with a loud sigh and eye roll that reminded him of Sage.

There were countless questions swirling in his head. He could ask outright about the Friends and their plans for the house, or if she'd overheard anything from Denise or the others about why Maude gave them the house. But that wasn't what came out of his mouth.

"Why don't you have a car?"

He thought it was a simple question, but the shock on Juliet's face had him fumbling to take it back.

"I'm sorry, you don't have to answer that—"

"No, it's fine."

"Is it claustrophobia?"

Shaking her head, Juliet let out a short, humorless chuckle. "That would be too easy. It's funny, actually. It's like something out of a reality TV show but when it's your life, it's way less entertaining."

Lucas held his breath while Juliet took a big one. Her words came out all in a rush, like she was ripping off a Band-Aid.

"My long-term boyfriend broke up with me on a four-hour drive home from a long weekend I thought he would use to propose."

That was not what Lucas had expected. "What a jerk. I hope you keyed that car when you got home."

His hand flexed on top of the closed book. Juliet's eyes lingered on it, instead of looking at him.

"Not exactly. It was my car. He was driving."

Her voice was thick, and she blinked a few times before looking away. The sun was beating down on the back of his neck and a bead of sweat trickled down his nose. He had no idea why she was being so open with him in person. She'd never even gotten close to this level of intimacy online, even though she was usually way more uninhibited with Plantsguy95.

No, that wasn't exactly true, now that he thought about it. She'd shared a lot at the fair, and so had he. What she shared online was more about work, not the more personal stuff he'd learned about her in the last few weeks. The quiet at the house had maybe been just that—quiet while they concentrated on getting through everything quickly, and not her withdrawing at something he'd said or done.

Whatever she was feeling, he was surprised to realize he'd rather have her share with him in person.

"He did it in *your* car?"

"Right at the start of the drive. He had a list of reasons he'd memorized and went through." A cloud shifted overhead and a beam of sunlight hit her face, illuminating the clammy paleness of it. "There were fifty-two of them."

The only way he was able to hide the hot, angry rage that bubbled up under his skin was by concentrating intently on that freckle right above her left eyebrow.

She inhaled a shaky breath. "The next few hours were not great, as you can imagine. Especially when his phone lit up with a text. The name of my best friend since high school—one of my only friends—popped up with a message."

"No."

"I told you, reality TV level stuff." She ran a hand through her hair. "It said, 'did you tell her yet? Can we finally be together?'"

Lucas cursed, and her eyes flicked to him.

"I'm sorry, but he has to be the absolute biggest piece of trash—" A few more swear words escaped and Juliet laughed, her eyes watery.

"You kiss your grandmother with that mouth?"

"I'm sure she'd have even worse to say if she heard about this jerk."

Her eyes widened, and he rushed to say, "But she won't ever hear it from me. No one will."

She took a deep breath and ran her hands through her hair again. "Anyway, to answer your question, I sold my car when I moved here, along with most of my stuff. I didn't want the memories."

"I totally get that."

"Do you?" She raised an eyebrow and took a sip of her drink. "You seem pretty intent on holding on tight to memories of Maude."

"Those are good ones."

Now she looked incredulous. "Every single memory in that house is a good one?"

"Is that your one question for answering one of mine?"

Her lips pulled up in a smirk. "You're avoiding answering me again."

"Is that really the one you want to ask?"

As she thought, she ran a finger over her lips. The move-

ment was absurdly distracting. He could see the careful calcula-
tion behind her eyes, the consideration she was giving to this,
the very important task of picking what she wanted to know
most about him.

As was becoming her habit, she surprised him.

"What do you think of *Pride and Prejudice?*"

There was the hint of something in her eyes when she
asked, a glimmer of hope, a desperate plea for acceptance. Did
she want him to like it?

When he found himself wanting to lie just to please her, he
knew he was in serious trouble.

He let out a breathy chuckle. "It's really boring."

Her mouth dropped open for a moment, but she quickly
snapped it shut. "Of course you would think that." She huffed
out a breath and leaned back in her chair, crossing her arms.

He threw his hands in the air. "All they do is go visit each
other and gossip about other people."

The smirk was back on her lips, and he liked seeing it there
way too much. "And how do you spend your time with your
family?"

Now it was his turn to drop his mouth open.

"Touché." He picked up the book and flipped through it.
"You've won this round, Miss Bingley."

"Bingley!" She looked outraged. "How on earth am I Caroline Bingley? She's everything Elizabeth isn't."

Though the temptation to take it all back and make her
smile was still there, this was way more fun.

They talked about books and kept annoying each other until
long past four o'clock. There had been plans Lucas had made
for his only day off that week, with the garden club, with his
family, but they were all forgotten in favor of spending time
with Juliet. Even though it was dangerous—or perhaps because
it was.

SIXTEEN

PLANTSGUY95

How's Pete doing?

Did he survive?

JCEDITS

Yes, he's doing fine.

PLANTSGUY95

And how are you?

JCEDITS

Nervous. Just about to send in my submission for the editing award. Two days before the deadline.

PLANTSGUY95

Exciting! When will you hear back?

JCEDITS

A few weeks.

PLANTSGUY95

Well, fingers crossed.

I'm sure your plants will appreciate the extra attention they'll be getting now.

JCEDITS

It wasn't that bad of a hermit phase this time.

The weather was good so I went to write outside.

PLANTSGUY95

That sounds nice.

JCEDITS

It was, but I had company.

PLANTSGUY95

Uh oh, don't tell me.

JCEDITS

Have you watched the movie yet?

PLANTSGUY95

Wow, so you've just totally abandoned any hope I'll read the book, huh?

JCEDITS

It's not for everyone.

I was bored the first time I read it in school. It gets better with the reread.

PLANTSGUY95

I'll have to trust you on that one.

It was only after Juliet had walked all the way to Cork and Beans that she realized she hadn't even told Charlotte about finishing up the magazine edits in time to send it in to BOC. Stopping in the middle of the sidewalk, she wondered what it meant that she'd told Plantsguy95 first. What he meant to her.

He couldn't mean anything, could he? That both felt dismissive and ridiculous at the same time. You could tell a lot about a person from the way they wrote. Plus he remembered things about her, and encouraged her.

Of course, Charlotte did that too.

Unlike Lucas.

Thinking about him was uncomfortable. The stubbornness he had about the house and dedication to the garden club was infuriating yet endearing. Had she ever cared about something that much? Not that she could remember. Not to the passionate, orange-tree stealing levels that Lucas did.

What she cared about most was finally doing something that grabbed her mother's attention, something that didn't involve her sending Juliet food because she'd forgotten to eat. What kind of person did that make Juliet, compared to the passionate, generous Lucas? Everything he did was for others: his grandmother, his family, the garden club, the town.

Suddenly irritated at him, even though he wasn't there, she stormed down the sidewalk. She was going to be late for her work session at Cork and Beans. He'd been right, of course, that she didn't reserve a table. She hadn't even spoken to the people who worked there, other than to order her drinks. They likely didn't even notice her.

That was what she wanted though, to fly under the radar, to avoid drama. Greenhaven was starting to feel comfortable, even as Lucas made her feel uncomfortable. It was just the right size for her car-less lifestyle, with everything she needed within reach. She felt safe, for the first time in a long time. Now she could think about putting herself back together after being shattered into a thousand tiny pieces that day in the car.

Telling Lucas about the previous week had opened something inside of her. He hadn't pressed for details, or assumed she'd done something wrong, the way so many people in her hometown had done. He was totally on her side in a way no one else had been in a long time. It was comfortable and uncomfortable all at once.

When she finally got to the café, it was already a quarter past the hour. She'd lost fifteen minutes to daydreaming about Plantsguy95 and Lucas.

When she stepped into the café, there was a familiar face behind the counter. Casey? Cassie?

"Juliet, hi." The woman smiled and held out a cup. "I got this all ready for you."

Too stunned to speak, Juliet just stood there, blinked at the cup in the woman's hand. After a moment, the woman's smile faded, and her cheeks started to turn red. "Um, did you want something else? You always get an oat milk latte when you come in at one on Wednesdays." She drew her hand back. "I can make you whatever you want."

"No." Juliet reached out and grabbed the cup. It was still piping hot, so she must have made it as soon as she saw her approaching on the sidewalk. Thickness settled in her throat and in her eyes. "It's perfect, thank you." She glanced down at the nametag on the woman's apron. "Carrie."

The woman's face lit up, and Juliet handed over a ten-dollar bill, more than enough for the five-dollar drink. The entirety of the change ended up in the cup next to the register.

Making her way to the back patio, she took a sip. A small sigh of happiness escaped her mouth. It was perfect. Just the same as it always was, just the way she liked it.

The patio, however, was not as Juliet liked it. Lucas was sitting at her table.

"No book today?" She was done feeling bad for this snark that seemed to pop up only for him. It was the biggest reason why he made her uncomfortable. He made her feel like someone else, someone . . . stronger.

"I finished it last night." He leaned back, the afternoon sun catching a few lighter strands in his hair and giving him a glow-ing, annoyingly angelic aura. "I have thoughts."

"And I have work to do. Can you save the thoughts until I'm done?"

"Of course."

He said it instantly, with no hint of sarcasm. That was the only reason she sat down and opened her laptop.

It was not because he'd left a muffin at the spot just across from him.

Juliet didn't really have that much work, now that the edits on the magazine had been sent to Denise and the BOC commit-tee. She wasn't about to say that to Lucas, of course. There were still things for her to plug away at, projects with looser deadlines that she could try to finish up. With her headphones in and the white noise app on maximum volume, it should have been easy enough to slip into one of her very focused states of concen-tration.

Instead, she found her eyes darting over to Lucas often enough that she lost her place in her document five times.

Once was known to happen occasionally. Twice if someone called or texted while she was working. But five times was just plain irritating.

Pulling her headphones out and dropping them on the table, she sighed.

"Fine, tell me your thoughts." She picked up the muffin and broke off a small piece.

He pulled his eyes away from his phone, a frown and furrowed brow still on his face. "Sorry, what?"

Juliet could feel her cheeks heat. "Never mind. I didn't mean to interrupt."

He put his phone into his pocket—not down on the table to glance at while they spoke—and gave her a smile. "Just a note from Sage about garden club business." His mouth twisted a little, like he didn't quite want to give more details. Then he did. "We may have found a new meeting space."

"That's great." A weight lifted off her shoulders she didn't realize had been there. Even though she knew it wasn't her responsibility, and Maude could do what she wanted with her own house, it was still awful Lucas had lost such a special place.

The club, she corrected herself. The whole garden club had lost it, not just Lucas.

"We'll see." He ran a hand through his hair again, and the air seemed to get caught somewhere in Juliet's upper chest. "You really want my thoughts on *Pride and Prejudice*?"

"Are they that bad?"

"Depends . . . is it bad if I stopped reading and just watched the movie?"

"Which one?" A bite-sized morsel of muffin made its way to her mouth.

"They made multiple movies of this book?" He looked completely flabbergasted.

Without meaning to, Juliet burst into laughter, almost choking on the muffin. It was something about his eyes being just a little too wide, and his mouth too perfect of a circle. Like he was a meme of a reaction instead of a real person.

"I watched the one with Keira Knightley."

"The correct one."

He wiped a hand over his forehead. "Phew."

"Well?" She broke off another piece of muffin.

"It's still just people going to visit each other and gossiping about other people." He leaned back in his chair and crossed his arms. "Elizabeth does not deserve Darcy."

Blood on fire, Juliet sat up straight, muffin forgotten. "I'm sorry, what?"

"She totally judged him based on that first interaction, never even thinking he might be ill at ease with new people. She never let him off the hook until he gave a bunch of money to help her family. And she ignored a perfectly acceptable potato-loving man because he was shorter than her." He took a sip of his drink. "She's terribly shallow."

Open-mouthed and speechless, Juliet stared at Lucas.

"But then Sage reminded me none of that matters."

A deep breath was required before she could respond. "Why not?"

"Because when you fall in love with someone, you fall in love with all of them, not just the good parts."

The words hung heavy in the air and stretched between them, tender and golden. Something that might have been hope glimmered in Juliet's chest.

She took a sip of her drink to break the silence before it got too awkward. "You watched it with your cousins?"

"Not all of them. Just the ones who would put up with all my questions and comments."

"So it wasn't like *Bachelor* night, then."

"How was that last night?"

"How did you know I went again?"

His eyebrow arched, teasing.

It was a ridiculous question. Of course one of his cousins had told him.

"It was good."

A second eyebrow raised to meet the first. Now he was incredulous.

Juliet laughed. "Yes, really. Your family is very nice."

They were all great, and it took all of her restraint not to tell him just how amazing it felt to have people be that nice to her again, after what she'd been through in her own hometown after the breakup.

Why did she keep telling him all these personal details? Even Charlotte didn't know this much about her life, and she'd been her friend for almost a decade. There was something about having his deep-brown eyes staring right into hers that made her want to crack open her chest and let everything gush out in a big puddle in front of her. It felt like he might not be totally disgusted by that.

He might be, though, despite what he'd realized while watching her favorite movie. And that was enough of a possibility to keep her holding back, just a little, so that she didn't end up without a car.

The car obviously being a metaphor for her heart. Juliet almost rolled her eyes at herself. She'd never see that kind of cheesy metaphor in a manuscript without calling it out.

"I'm glad you think my family's nice." Lucas's words pulled her out of her thoughts.

"You don't?"

"They can be . . . intense."

"I thought they were the most important thing to you." She leaned back and picked at her muffin.

"They are, but I'm starting to wonder if we're too involved in each other's lives."

Now he was sharing something with her. A bubbling excitement made its way through her stomach to her chest. Unsure of how to do this kind of thing in person rather than from behind a screen, she asked the question that had been buzzing around her head for weeks.

"Are they part of your plan to get back the house, now that we're all done cleaning it out?"

His eyes cut to hers, intense and focused. "They haven't told you?"

She shook her head. "All we talked about is *The Bachelor*."

He seemed surprised at that, as if used to people sharing private details about him when he wasn't there. Then his expression closed off, and he pulled out his phone to look at the screen. "I'm sorry, I have to go meet Sage."

Trying not to let her disappointment show, she gave him a smile and popped her earphones back in. Once again, she'd managed to say the wrong thing, but there wasn't the overwhelming sense of failure like she usually had. Just a lingering urge to see him again, on purpose.

Which was so much more dangerous.

SEVENTEEN

JCEDITS

So, um, I'm a finalist for the editing award.

PLANTSGUY95

What? That's amazing!

JCEDITS

Thanks.

PLANTSGUY95

Is there an awards ceremony, like the Oscars?

JCEDITS

Actually, yes.

PLANTSGUY95

Lol, I was just kidding, but wow, okay, awesome.

JCEDITS

I don't think I'll go.

PLANTSGUY95

I'm sure you'll win.

JCEDITS

It's not that. it's just far away.

PLANTSGUY95

You always said what you like most about your
job is that you can do it anywhere.

JCEDITS

When did I say that?

PLANTSGUY95

I dunno, a post a while ago.

JCEDITS

You read all my posts?

PLANTSGUY95

You mean you don't read all of mine?

JCEDITS

Only the ones I don't edit to see what mistakes
you made, haha.

Looking around the room full of people munching on carrot sticks and ranch, the walls ablaze with colorful artwork, Lucas felt the distinct urge to back out of the room slowly. The only reason he was at the art show, dressed in an itchy, expensive suit he'd worn maybe five times total in his life, was for Granny.

Every year a member of the garden club—Maude or Granny —bid on at least a few paintings as part of the art school's fundraiser. They'd both taken classes when they were younger, and so had Lucas and all his cousins. Horticultural drawing was something a lot of the garden club enjoyed, even if Lucas's talents weren't exactly what one would call well-developed.

Some of his first posts on his Plantsguy95 account had been drawings, quickly deleted.

Most of those first posts had been deleted, in fact, none of them good enough for the person he'd originally created the account to impress.

That person was the reason he didn't want to be here tonight.

And that person was heading right toward him.

"Lucas, how nice to see you."

At the sound of his ex's voice, the hair on Lucas's neck stood up.

"Hi, Audrey." His smile was small and forced, but he had to smile. What other choice did he have? Anything he said or did that was even a little impolite would get back to Granny. Even if Audrey had never liked his family, never even tried to get to know them, that didn't mean Granny would want him to be rude to her. "How have you been?"

"Not bad." Her eyes raked up and down his body. "You're looking well."

Looks were what mattered most to Audrey. Her golden curls were smooth and frizz-free, her skin flawlessly contoured, and her dress was the exact right balance between revealing too much and too little skin. This sheen of perfection was all thanks to a routine that Lucas knew took several hours per day and a closet full of products that all cost more than his suit.

Considering how much of his day Lucas spent on his own interests—and how much green he laid out on plants—he didn't judge what others did with their time and money. His curious mind liked when someone could teach him something new. But Audrey wasn't interested in teaching, only directing, and she never held back her judgment of anyone or anything. Her gaze lingered on his suit and she must be thinking his situation had changed since she dumped him two years ago.

"Thanks."

"I wasn't expecting to see you tonight." Audrey bit her lip, a well-rehearsed move. Compared to Juliet, whose unpracticed and unconscious nervous tic made his pulse race, Audrey doing the same thing turned him ice cold. "Did you come here just to see little ol' me?"

"I'm here because Granny couldn't come. I'm here for the club."

That did nothing to deter Audrey. "Hopefully we can catch up later."

"Catch up about what?"

Not even flustered, she said, "I'd love to hear what you've been up to. Sounds like you're doing a lot online these days."

Of course it was about his account. The same one he'd started to impress her. At first, she'd liked what all his work in landscaping did to his muscles, but she hadn't liked the look of him as just an employee in a store in town. She'd always pushed him to do more, become a manager, start his own company, something that would look better.

Look better to who, he wasn't sure. Her friends, her family, the world. He hadn't put his face on the account initially in order to make it a surprise for her. She'd dumped him long before he'd had enough of a following to be impressive.

Though apparently it was big enough now to be worthy of her attention.

"I'm doing okay. I like helping people with their plants."

"Your last post seemed to get a lot of shares. Are you getting sponsored now?"

Holy Hoya, this was not the conversation he wanted to be having right now.

Suddenly he felt a hand on his arm. "There you are, darling, I was looking everywhere for you."

A warm flood of relief made its way through his body when he heard Juliet's voice. Now her head was resting on his shoulder, and his heart wanted to thump itself right out of his body.

"This is Juliet Chapman, my . . . " With a chuckle, he trailed off and looped an arm over her shoulders to squeeze her tight. "Well, no words can really describe who she is to me."

The words had felt like the least untruthful thing he could say, but he didn't realize just how true they were until he'd said them. How *would* he describe her if he had to? Rival community organization member? Careful preserver of his family's precious memories? Secret online crush who he still hadn't revealed himself to?

That last thought almost had his smile faltering. With Juliet, he still had one gigantic untruth that had been slowly eating away at him more and more as the weeks went by.

Now that his original plan wasn't going to work, there was no reason to keep it from her anymore. No reason other than the woman standing in front of them, her nose turned up and critical eyes taking in Juliet's outfit.

Lucas had already lost someone once because of Plantsguy95. In the end, and with lots of input from his cousins, he knew he was better off without Audrey. Juliet was different though. The thought of her rejecting him, of pushing him away because of his online persona made his chest burn.

Though right now a very different part of his body was burning thanks to her arm wrapped around his waist.

"There's a painting I think you should buy." Juliet pulled herself out of his one-armed embrace and tugged at his hand. "It was nice to meet you . . . ?" She smiled at the other woman.

"Audrey."

"Nice to meet you Avery." The deliberate mispronunciation was delivered with such effortless charm, Lucas wasn't sure who was more surprised, him or Audrey.

Once they'd made their way through the maze of rooms to one that was empty of people, Juliet dropped his hand like it was on fire. "I'm sorry. It looked like you could use some saving back there. I hope I didn't overstep and you actually did want to talk to her."

He flexed his fingers, his arm still missing the outline of her body against his. "I definitely didn't want to talk to her. She's an ex."

Juliet's eyebrows shot up, the question clear on her face. It was hard to say more, even though Juliet had told him a lot about her love life. When she'd told him, it was because he'd asked about her not having a car. If he told her now, it would be like admitting he wanted her to know he was definitely single, which she had never asked outright. Still, he had to say something.

"She didn't dump me in my car or anything."

"It doesn't have to be in a car to hurt."

Lucas ran a hand through his hair and looked around the room. It was one of the smaller meeting rooms in the community center, the chairs and tables removed for the night so that the art on the walls would be more visible. But all Lucas could see was Juliet. "She didn't really like my job."

"At the hardware store?" Juliet moved toward the closest drawing and leaned in to examine it with her sharp eyes. "Why not?"

With her gaze on something other than him, and the room empty of other people, the words flowed a little easier. He crossed his arms and glanced briefly at the drawing next to Juliet. "Back then, I was working at the supermarket. I've hopped around, worked everywhere in town. I do a lot of landscaping in the summer for people."

"That's impressive."

"Really?"

She turned back to look at him and gave him a small shrug. "Yeah. You know everyone in town, they know you. You're able to help whoever needs it most."

A breath caught in his throat. That was exactly why he did it. Audrey had never understood that, not in the two years they'd been together, and Juliet got it after only knowing him a month.

Though technically, she'd known him a lot longer. She just didn't realize it yet.

Snapdragon, he really had to tell her soon.

"I mean, she liked the bod I got from all that work outside." He uncrossed his arms and put his hands on his hips, liking the way her eyes followed the movement. "But she wanted me to become a manager, or start a business and work for myself like you do."

He didn't know if it was the compliment about her job or the comment on his body that prompted her cheeks to turn bright pink. She returned her eyes to the next drawing on the wall. Normally he'd have enjoyed making her squirm, but tonight felt different. She'd helped him out, so she deserved a little more information about who Audrey was.

"She was also super snobby about my family, even though they were beyond nice to her." It wasn't just Lucas who wasn't enough for her, in the end. "The complicated, mixed-up lives of the Geis family were just too much for her."

"Well then, I'm glad I interrupted."

"Me too. You were amazing."

"I know, right?" This compliment had her grinning, and she swept her hair over her shoulder, an adorable little preening moment. "I've never done anything like that before. All my practice being rude to you has paid off, it seems. Now I can be rude to anyone. Except your grandmother, of course."

He laughed, and he looked around the room. It was filled with drawings from one of the beginner classes. "Was there really a painting you wanted me to buy? That's why I'm here, after all."

"Really?"

"The garden club buys a few every year."

"I thought Maude painted all of those in her house. I was wondering why you didn't push for any of them. Now I know."

He tilted his head to look at the one in front of them. "I mean, it's certainly . . . creative."

They looked at each other and burst into laughter. Juliet wiped a tear from her eye and looked around the room. "They're all braver than me, that's for sure. Putting your art out there like that."

"And risk being ridiculed by the very savvy art connoisseurs in this town?"

"I'm sure they're just horrified we don't understand this abstract interpretation of, um," She leaned in and looked at the little tag with the title. "A Britney Spears concert." Her eyes widened. "Is that what her concerts are like?"

"Maybe for this person." He chuckled and they fell into a comfortable silence, taking in the drawings. He took a deep breath. "I think you're pretty brave."

Still looking at the art, she waved a hand. "I just edit other people's bravery. It's easy to tell people what's not working. Easy to spot the mistakes when it's not your blood, sweat, and tears on the page." She paused and shifted. A spotlight meant for the amateur drawings on the walls hit her hair, turning it fire red for an instant. "It does feel amazing, though, helping them make it better. Even when it's just a technical handbook. I make sure it's not confusing, and there's no misplaced punctuation that might render it ineffective."

Warmth hit his chest. "I had no idea you were so passionate about it."

It wasn't that Lucas was surprised, exactly, but this passion wasn't something that came across as much in her social media. She was very businesslike in her posts, highlighting the advantages of working with an editor and explaining the different services she provided.

Her eyes flicked away from his and she tucked a strand of hair behind her ear, dark reddish again without the spotlight on it. "I wouldn't have been doing it for over a decade if I wasn't."

"The only thing I've done for that long is keep a bonsai tree alive."

She turned to him, humor sparkling in her eyes.

"That's certainly worthy of some sort of prize."

"You must have a ton of prizes for your work."

She got quiet, all of a sudden, closing up tighter than a tulip at night.

Too close, he told himself. He wasn't supposed to know that much about her work, not offline.

"There's this editing award I'm a finalist for." Her eyes were still fixed on the painting in front of them, but her cheeks had taken on a slightly pink tinge. "With a dinner and awards ceremony next week during the annual conference."

"That's amazing. Congratulations." Though he'd written the words to her before, saying them out loud, then seeing her cheeks flush and eyes sparkle at the praise was even better. "Will it be a fun-filled evening like this?"

His poor attempt at humor may have covered any lack of surprise in his voice, but it only got him half a smile from Juliet.

"I'm not going."

"Why not?"

She shrugged. Maybe this was something too personal, for either Plantsguy95 or Lucas to know.

"Won't there be a bunch of other editors so you can geek out over commas or whatever?"

There was a little upward tilt of her lips. "I have one friend who was going but her husband had something come up, and

I'm not going to go on my own. Besides, I don't—" She bit her lip.

"You don't think you'll win?"

Her eyes flicked to his. "It's a six-hour drive."

"Oh."

Little bursts of happy bubbles made their way from his belly up into his chest and throat. She hadn't told Plantsguy95 that. He liked the idea that she may prefer Lucas to someone online, even one she shared a lot with.

Which was the only reason he could think of that the next words out of his mouth were, "I could drive you, if you want. You helped me out tonight, after all."

Now she turned her head completely to look at him, eyes wide and eyebrows sky high.

"We can barely stand next to each other for more than five minutes without needling each other, and you want to drive me to the other side of the state just to thank me for getting you out of a conversation with your ex?"

"To be fair, I think the art is what's getting most of our needling tonight."

This time, instead of even a half smile, he got pursed lips and downcast eyes from her.

"Why would you help me?"

Because I feel horribly guilty about how much I've been lying to you, was what he wanted to say. He had to tell her. Soon. Maybe even tonight.

Sage and Heather would do it in a few weeks no matter what, but he knew it had to be him. Maybe when she found out that she knew him better than she realized, she'd like him, really like him.

Or she'd hate him forever.

Instead of answering, he did what he knew would annoy

her, and answered her question with one of his own. "Do you know why I'm here tonight?"

She sighed and rolled her eyes. "Because there's nothing to plant and you're bored?"

"Granny and Maude helped found the art school in town."

"Oh."

"Horticulture art is something the garden club has always enjoyed, and what started as bringing in a drawing teacher for the club turned into much larger classes for the town."

Turning her attention back to the painting, she brought a hand to her hair and twisted a dark reddish strand around her finger. "That's fascinating."

"We help each other in this town. All the different groups. We bid on their paintings, and they buy at our plant sale." He nudged her shoulder with his to get her to look at him. "Everyone buys books from the Friends. Where do you think I got that copy of *Pride and Prejudice?*"

"We could listen to the audiobook while we drive if you want."

"Just for that, I'm going to rescind my offer."

She laughed now, finally, and he relaxed. "Thank you, that's very generous. I'll think about it."

He cleared his throat. "You really did save me back there with Audrey. I'd like to repay that somehow."

Frowning, she cut her eyes to his. "There are easier ways than a six-hour drive."

That should have been enough, but he wanted to be sure she went to that event. Before tonight, she'd never talked about her work with Lucas. Maybe there was something about him that made her embarrassed about what she did. Just like he sometimes wondered if Audrey had been right, that he lacked ambition, which wasn't a thought he liked to share with people.

"It's amazing how you're running your own business."

She waved that away. "Lots of people do that."

"Well, I don't. Even tried once and failed." There was more to the story, so much more, but he wanted to make sure she felt proud of her own work. He cleared his throat. "I know how hard it is. You've been doing it for years, too, so it's great there's an award you'll be able to show off to your mom."

Too close again. Sharp alert pierced his chest. He should really just tell her. Then he wouldn't have to keep straight what she'd told him in person and what she'd only told him online.

She inhaled deeply and peeked up at him. "You might drive me all the way there and I could end up losing. I don't want to waste your time."

"Getting to spend some time with you won't be a waste."

Now her breathing stopped completely and her wide eyes locked with his. "Do you really mean that?"

He took a step toward her, his palm itching to touch her face, her arm, anywhere.

"Absolutely."

She licked her lips and took a step toward him—

"Shrimp?"

They both jumped back, and turned to see a server standing next to them with a tray on an outstretched hand. When they shook their heads, he wandered out of the room, leaving them alone.

Turning toward each other again, Lucas took another small step toward Juliet right as she did the same. Their arms and shoulders bumped gently, and they chuckled nervously, but neither of them moved back. The sweet smell of paint and ink filled the air around them, and the only sound was her breath coming in short little gasps.

In the space of a heartbeat, she leaned in and kissed him.

Her lips were warm and electric, the tingling sensation starting at his mouth and quickly consuming his entire body. It was the very last thing he'd expected, yet suddenly was the only thing he wanted to do for the rest of his life. Her hands were in his hair, pulling him to her, breathing him in like oxygen, setting him on fire. Their lips met again and again, their tongues dancing, slowly at first, then more intensely.

Without even trying, she'd worked her way into his brain, his life, every part of her intriguing and infuriating, none of it boring or predictable. Every single part of him wanted every single part of her.

Which was why when he brought up his hands, instead of lacing them around her, holding her tight and never letting go, he put them on her shoulders and gently pushed away.

She didn't know who he was. Not all of him.

He had to tell her who he was. He had to tell her that she knew more about him than she realized, had seen parts of him no one else ever had. That he knew just how much he'd irritated her when they'd first met, and how funny she was in person and online.

He took a step back and dropped his arms, searching for the right words.

The second he opened his mouth to admit everything, she turned on her heel and ran out of the room.

EIGHTEEN

The cool evening air slapped Juliet in the face, heating her cheeks even more than the blazing fire they already were. The only sounds in the familiar—and thankfully empty—street she was running down were the distant whoosh of cars on the highway and the pounding of her heart in her ears. The same silent houses from a few weeks before were now openly mocking her, their windows like eyes lit up with laughter.

When compared to being dumped at the start of a four-hour car ride, someone pushing away from a kiss shouldn't have been a big deal. Especially someone she'd been so thoroughly convinced she didn't even like that much.

Except she did like Lucas. She liked him enough to save him from what had looked like a horribly awkward conversation. She liked him enough to consider braving another long car ride with him when she didn't even like short ones with her mom. She liked him enough to tell him things she never told anyone else.

The pain in her chest was so strong, Juliet had to stop running to sit down on a bench and catch her breath. With her eyes closed, she inhaled, the air crisp in her lungs, and her heart rate slowed.

When she opened her eyes, her heart stopped. She'd picked the bench across the street from the Periwinkle Mansion.

"Juliet."

Lucas was out of breath, coming down the street. In an instant, Juliet was on her feet, walking away from him.

"Juliet, please slow down."

Nope, not happening. This time, she would be the one in control, the one to walk away.

"I just want to talk."

"I don't really feel like talking."

"Then I'll wait until you do."

She shot another look behind her and instantly softened. Rather than his usual smirk on his lips or glittering humor in his eyes, he looked completely earnest. For whatever reason, he wanted to give her details on why he wasn't interested.

Maybe he wasn't over Audrey, even if the woman hadn't been that nice to his family. It would be understandable—Audrey was gorgeous. Juliet looked down at the simple blouse and dark pants she'd pulled out for the art auction. It was the kind of boring, safe, predictable outfit she'd always preferred. The kind The Ex had mentioned in his hours-long monologue about all the reasons Juliet's ex-best friend was a better match for him.

Tonight, she'd actually managed to forget about that for a few hours. For once, she'd been excited to venture out and be social. Denise had sent around an email earlier in the day to all the Friends volunteers reminding them of the art show. It seemed like a good way to thank Denise in person for letting her submit her work on the library's lit magazine to the BOC, especially since she was now a finalist.

Juliet hadn't planned on running into Lucas there. Or kissing him.

Heat crept up her skin again. Still clueless as to what had

possessed her to do such a thing, she increased the pace of her steps. Even so, she could hear him not far behind her, his pace matching hers.

He didn't say anything else, just kept following her as she made her way through the dark streets toward her apartment. When she got there, he sat down on the bench across the street while she dug in her purse for her keys. It was the bench for the bus stop. A bus she'd never taken because of a cruel man who'd broken her heart in a moving vehicle and made her hate the feeling of being trapped in one with no way out.

This wasn't heartbreak, she told herself as she unlocked the front door and stepped inside the vestibule. This was just a misunderstanding between people who were kind of friends but mostly got on each other's nerves. And who also told each other a lot of personal stuff for reasons she didn't completely understand.

It was that mysterious connection that had made her lose her mind for a minute and kiss him. It had been a long time since someone had opened up to her. She wasn't falling for him, she was just out of practice talking to people in person and had gotten overwhelmed.

She could still see him through the window. He wasn't on his phone, or looking up around. His gaze was on the front door, patient, remorseful. Those eyes of his, even from across the street, could tell her so much.

Maybe he was over Audrey but had a girlfriend . . . that he'd never mentioned in the hours they'd spent together cleaning out Maude's house.

Or, more realistically, he didn't know how to nicely say he didn't like her like that. She hadn't even realized she liked him that much until he'd pushed her away and instead of mild disappointment, there'd been a hot burst in her chest like she'd been punched.

Looking around the vestibule and the tidy row of mailboxes, she wished she had someone to talk to about these kinds of things. When The Ex had left, he'd taken her best friend with him. Who, Juliet had later realized, had been using all her questions and complaining as ammunition against her, as a way to win over her boyfriend.

There was a brief thought that she might be able to talk to Mari about Lucas. But this was way beyond the scope of their budding friendship and felt almost like cheating. Juliet could ask Mari for insight into Lucas, but he had no way to find out more about her through back channels. She took out her phone and stared at it, going through the very small list of people she was regularly in touch with.

Her mother was obviously not an option. Neither was her sister. She briefly considered her brother-in-law, but since most of their conversations over the years had been about his most recent triathlon, they didn't exactly have that kind of background that lent itself to brotherly advice.

Her finger hovered over Plantsguy95. Though things had slowly been getting more personal, this felt too personal. Also, for reasons she would explore later, she didn't want him to know she'd kissed anyone. It didn't feel like cheating, just . . . something she didn't want him to know about.

Charlotte's name was right under his. Something about her felt safe. They'd already talked about guys—well, Plantsguy95—and Charlotte had been with her husband since they were high school sweethearts. While she didn't mention him often in their chats about editing, whenever she did, she sounded happy. While the fear of a second rejection in one night loomed large, it felt worse to leave Lucas sitting outside all night, not knowing what he might be thinking about her and the kiss.

Instead of a message, Juliet pulled up Charlotte's phone number and called.

"Juliet! What's wrong?"

"Um, hi." Juliet took a deep breath and leaned against the wall in the vestibule. "How did you know something was wrong?"

"You only call when you're worried about a client or deadline. Is there something I can take off your plate?"

Warmth flooded her chest. Charlotte hadn't even hesitated. She might once she heard what Juliet was struggling with, but at least her first reaction hadn't been dismissive.

"It's not work, it's something personal. I know that's not what we usually talk about—"

"Are you okay? Did something happen with your family?"

"No, it's not that. It's a, um, guy situation."

"You mean a love problem?" Charlotte sounded thrilled. "Charlie, get over here. Juliet's having a man issue."

Turning away from the row of mailboxes and the window that framed Lucas's sitting form, Juliet's pulse kicked up and climbed the stairs to her apartment. This wasn't a conversation she wanted to have where one of her neighbors might hear. She wasn't even sure *she* wanted to hear this conversation.

"It's not a big deal." She unlocked her front door and made her way into her living room, turning on lamps as she went. "You don't need to bother your husband."

"I may understand *The Chicago Manual of Style*, but it has been almost two decades since I've been on a first date. I have no idea how men's brains work these days."

"Why do you think I know?" A deep voice joined the call, presumably Charlie.

Charlie and Charlotte. It was so adorable, it was ridiculous.

"You have brothers, you have friends. You hear them talk about women."

"You want me to tell you what they say?" He sounded horrified.

"No, just listen to Juliet's problem and give her your opinion as a man."

A loud sigh from Charlie must have meant yes. If she weren't so nervous, Juliet would have been laughing. It was nice to see another side of Charlotte. Reading a few lines about her husband wasn't the same as actually hearing them together. It made Juliet ache to think she might never have that. That something was so wrong with her, and she'd always keep getting pushed away. She sank onto the couch and pulled a blanket over her lap.

"So what's got you stuck?" Charlotte asked.

"There's this guy—"

"Plantsguy95?" she shrieked.

"Honey, let her talk."

"I'm sorry, she's just been chatting with this guy online for months and—"

"It's not him," Juliet said. "It's someone in town."

"Oh, even better."

"Not really. It's a smallish town, so I see him everywhere, and we were stuck together to clean out this house . . . " Juliet shook her head, even though they couldn't see her. "It doesn't really matter. What matters is I kissed him tonight, and he pushed me away. But then he ran after me and now he's sitting outside my apartment building, waiting to talk to me."

Charlie spoke first, his voice serious. "Did he push you, like shove? Or more a nudge?"

Ever the editor, Charlotte added, "Word choice is very important here."

Her hand not holding the phone clenched around the blanket on her lap. Even though every part of her wanted to pretend it never happened, Juliet thought back to that horrible moment less than an hour ago. The feel of his hand on her shoulder, the excitement that had bubbled up in her stomach at his touch and then . . . the crash of disappointment. "He put his hands on my shoulders, and I thought he was going to put them around me, but instead he dropped them and just kind of, stepped back."

"And then what?"

"And then I ran out of the building."

"He didn't say anything?"

"I didn't really give him a chance." No sense giving him time to say something like "I don't like you that way" or "I have a girlfriend."

Charlotte seemed to be thinking the same thing. "Does he have a girlfriend?"

"Not that I know of. I haven't outright asked him though."

"Where were you when you kissed?" Charlie asked.

Juliet leaned back and rested her head on the arm of the couch. "At an art show."

"That sounds very romantic." Charlotte sighed.

"He doesn't have a girlfriend." Charlie's voice was strong, and certain. "He just didn't want to make out in front of people."

That seemed . . . reasonable. And probably something Juliet should have thought of herself. But with Lucas, her brain didn't work in its usual way. It short circuited, made her say things and do things she almost never did. Like just the sight of him, the smell of him, the feel of him in the room, made everything else fade away. Even now, she could feel him sitting outside, shifting on the uncomfortable wooden bench. She didn't even have to look out the window to check, though she stood up from the couch and looked, just in case.

He was still there, one elbow on his knee and his head in his hand, looking miserable.

"He's still outside."

"Is he on his phone?"

"No."

"He definitely doesn't have a girlfriend." Charlie sounded more sure than when Juliet walked a client through the proper use of semicolons. "It's a Friday night and he was at an artsy event. If he hadn't brought his girlfriend with him, he'd have gone there right after."

"Like when you'd have those boring sport ball things in college and instead of partying with your friends after, you'd come back to my dorm room."

"You mean the Division I football games I was kicker for?"

"Ugh, yes, they were always so long."

Juliet almost didn't want to interrupt. Her weekly *Bachelor* viewing had exponentially increased her appreciation for this kind of rehearsed, repetitive drama. "So, should I go out there and talk to him?"

"Yes!" Charlotte and Charlie cried in unison.

Well, that was as unambiguous an answer as she could have hoped for.

She said goodbye and promised to update them once it was over.

Before heading out there, however, Juliet took her time braiding her hair, then taking out her contacts, and finally, brushing her teeth. If this went badly, she didn't want to cry herself to sleep without taking care of basic hygiene.

At the door, Juliet paused and took a deep breath before stepping into the night.

The instant she was across the street, Lucas stood up, hands raised, expression desperate.

"I am so sorry I upset you."

"I appreciate that." She waited. He wanted to talk. That didn't mean she had to.

There was a long pause, and he swept a hand down his face. "I stepped away because . . . you don't really know me."

She opened her mouth to say that wasn't true, then closed it. He was right. They had only spoken a few times about deeper topics, and she'd shared way more than he had. A slight flicker of worry went through her and she took a step back. The single streetlight in front of her building suddenly seemed inadequate against the heavy darkness of the night. "You mean like, you're actually a serial killer and I should stay away?"

He raised an eyebrow. "You think I could get away with anything like that with my cousins?"

Despite everything, she smiled at that. "They don't gossip about you with me, you know. We only talk about *The Bachelor* when I'm there."

He raised the other eyebrow, incredulous. "I find that extremely hard to believe. They literally talk nonstop about everybody all the time."

"Even me?" Unease settled in her chest. Was this just like her former best friend, but times eight? Another step back. She was almost in the street.

He held out a hand. "No, not like that. They just say how sweet you are."

"So they do talk about me." Tears prickled at the edges of her eyes. After everything that had happened after the breakup, the gossip around town, it was the thing Juliet was most afraid of. Gossip, people talking about her when she wasn't there. It all eventually led to isolation, and not the self-chosen kind.

With a frustrated grunt, Lucas stabbed both of his hands into his hair and walked back and forth around the bench. Juliet was suddenly acutely aware of all the muscles on his body, and how massive they were in comparison to hers. She spent her days sitting in front of a computer, and all the walks around town and carrying home bags of oranges couldn't compare to Lucas, who used every single one of his muscles every day. The body he'd so casually mentioned at the art show was on full display beneath the tight, dark suit he had on.

Instead of feeling afraid about arguing with a tall, brawny man on a dark street, she focused on his body, and how smoothly he moved in tight little circles around the bus stop bench, careful never to get too close to her. Juliet felt safe. His entire life was about protecting people, taking care of them. There was no built-up tension in his muscles, only restrained security, looking for whatever danger threatened Juliet. Right now, it was his own inability to communicate whatever he was trying to say, and whatever hesitation she'd felt melted away.

She took a step toward him. "Why is it so important that I know you before I can kiss you?"

He let out a heavy sigh and looked at her, his eyes full of regret she didn't fully understand. "It doesn't seem fair when I know so much about you."

"Do you want me to get to know you?"

"More than anything."

The intensity of his gaze promised much more than a kiss and had heat flooding her body.

With a shaky breath to calm her racing heart, she took another step toward him. "Then drive me to the BOC gala."

Wary happiness streaked across his face. "Really?"

She nodded, swallowing hard. The desire to spend the time with him was stronger than the dread of whatever uncomfortable awkwardness it might also incite. Only a tiny bit stronger, but it was enough for now. "We'll have six hours in the car to get to know each other. Horrible taste in music and everything."

"I have excellent taste in music."

"That's not what Heather said."

He gasped, placing a dramatic hand on his chest. "You said they don't talk about me."

Juliet giggled. "Well, they didn't pull out baby pictures or anything. But some stuff slips in there."

"If you want baby pictures, I'll see what I can find before the trip."

The heaviness lifted away from them both, and they fell back into their easy, playful banter. He didn't stay much longer, just long enough to work out the details of when he'd pick her up the following week.

Just long enough for hope to spark a fire in Juliet's chest that kept her from falling asleep until late into the night.

NINETEEN

Even though it was close to fifty years old, his truck smelled like a new car. Lucas wasn't sure if that would help Juliet's uncomfortable feelings associated with moving vehicles, but it couldn't hurt. Especially since it had smelled like dirt and fertilizer before. It was a smell Lucas appreciated, Audrey had hated, and everyone else in his life seemed indifferent about. Even with Juliet's love of plants, he didn't think she'd appreciate smelling cow manure for six hours.

Pulling up in front of her apartment building, he wasn't sure if he should get out and knock on her door, like this was a date, or honk, like he was just a friend picking her up. Then he remembered this was the twenty-first century and reached for his phone to send her a message, pulse racing at the sight of her name. They hadn't spoken since the night of the art show. He also hadn't messaged JC, deciding he wouldn't talk to her online until she knew the truth. Which would be very soon.

From the corner of his eye, a curtain flickered.

Great, now Angela Relish, Mari's friend, had seen him. He might as well get out of the car. By the time he drove off, all of his cousins would know he'd been here.

Just as he opened his car door, Juliet stepped out of her building. She had a small duffle bag in her hand, and a dress in dry-cleaning plastic.

Lucas could practically feel Angela's eyes boring into him from her second-floor window.

On cue, his phone dinged, and a glance down told him it was Mari. Another ding and Sage's name appeared on his screen as well.

He ignored them both to smile at Juliet. "Need any help?"

She shook her head, and blushed. Avoiding his eyes, she reached for the door handle, which he managed to grab at the same time. The brush of his hand against hers was electric, and he inhaled sharply just as she did. There was a moment when their eyes met, and the full weighty potential of this trip settled deep into his belly.

Juliet blinked and the spell was broken.

He opened the car door and she cleared her throat. "Thanks."

"I'm at your service today. Whatever you need to stay calm before your big night." He winced. That was probably the cheesiest thing he'd ever said. At least Angela could only see him from her window, not hear him.

Cheesy or not, Juliet gave him a small, sad smile in response. "The only way to stay calm is to not go."

She stepped up into the truck, and he shut the door, ran to his side, and got in as fast as he could. The sooner they were moving, the sooner he had an excuse to not respond to his cousins.

Settling himself behind the wheel, he wanted to make sure she still wanted this. "If you really don't want to go, you don't have to."

Her eyes flicked back to her apartment. There seemed to be

an internal debate raging, and her teeth worried her bottom lip so hard, he worried she'd draw blood.

Then you can kiss it and make her feel better.

No, this trip wasn't about that. This was to help her, and for her to get to know him, nothing more.

After a moment, she set her jaw and turned back to him. "I want to go. I want—" She ducked her head. "I want my mom to see a picture of me there. Even if I don't win, to see me there at a gala . . . that'll mean something to her."

Lucas almost nodded before he realized this was the first time she'd told him in person about wanting her mom's approval. "Doesn't owning your own business mean something to her?"

Juliet shrugged, and he pulled away from the curb.

"It's not like being a lawyer, like my sister."

"Sibling rivalry." Lucas hummed sagely, flipping on his blinker to turn toward the road that led out of town. "I can totally get that. Definitely worth six hours in the car with someone you don't particularly like just to prove you're the best kid of the bunch."

Juliet laughed, and the tension eased from Lucas's shoulders a little.

"This vintage truck is enchanting but are you sure it can make the trip?"

He smiled and shook his head. They were back in teasing territory again. "Only two minutes in and you're already insulting my ride." There was a bump in the road that rattled the interior of the seats. "It was my grandad's."

"Oh, wow, I didn't realize." The worn leather squeaked as she shifted positions. "I'm sorry."

He let her squirm another minute before chuckling. "Don't be. It was a total wreck before. He hated it and was going to take it to the dump before I saved it."

She reached over and shoved him in the arm. "You jerk."

"How was *The Bachelor* last night?"

"Didn't Sage or Mari tell you?"

"Tell me what?"

With that, she launched into a play-by-play of a very intense fight between Lily and Ivy. Apparently his twin cousins had both bought their twin boys the same outfit, and they both refused to return it.

It was silly family stuff, but Juliet told the story like it was just as dramatic as the reality show they were all there to watch.

Lucas shook his head and chuckled. "They'll forget about it by next week. That's how they are."

"I don't know, they seemed pretty mad."

"You don't fight with your sister?"

"We don't really see each other enough to have anything to fight about."

There was a lingering sadness underneath her light words, that he decided not to dig into right now. They were barely twenty minutes into this drive. There would be time to go deeper later.

"Well, nobody told me about their fight." He glanced at her. "Probably because they knew you'd tell me today."

Another squeak from the seat told him she was squirming again. "They know you're driving me?"

"Not exactly." Sage would have had a field day if she'd heard he was driving Juliet so far away. Already his cousins had welcomed her into their little group, with much more enthusiasm than they'd ever shown Audrey or any of his other girl-friends.

Whether Juliet realized it or not, it was a really big deal. It didn't seem like she had many friends in real life, and to have eight all at once would probably overwhelm her. It was better for her to think they were just being polite.

"They only know I'm helping you with something. This is your thing. I wouldn't tell anyone about it if you didn't want me to."

He glanced over at her, and she gave him a small, soft smile. "Thank you. I know it must be hard to keep something from them. You're all so close and share so much."

"A break from them isn't the worst thing, trust me."

He'd been thinking about that a lot, actually, for the last few weeks. Their lives were so intertwined, their opinions given so freely about each other's activities, that it could get stifling at times.

When Audrey had pointed this out, he'd cut them off as she'd requested but been miserable the whole time. There'd never been any effort from her to try things his way, she just assumed her way was better.

"It's nice how you all spend so much time together. How you all support each other." She turned to look out the window and watch the passing trees. "That's what family should do."

Lucas wasn't sure if Granny and Sage would call his recent crusade over the new garden club headquarters "support." They had a meeting space leased, some boring, bland conference room in a town building. This weekend should have been spent plotting how to turn things around and drafting a new petition to Mayor Taylor.

Instead, he was on a road trip with Juliet.

"Did your mom not support you after the breakup?" His gut clenched. "I'm sorry, that's a super personal question. You don't have to answer it."

"Isn't that why we're here? To get to know each other better?"

She kept her gaze out the window, however, and Lucas kept his on the road.

"She did, in her way. My sister had just had her second baby though, so she wasn't there a lot. And people around town were . . . " Juliet trailed off and he turned his head to look at her. Her eyebrows were twisted up tight, and she licked her lips before continuing. "It was all they could talk about. Whenever anyone stopped me, they said how sorry they were, but then they'd walk away and I'd overhear how they'd always thought he fit better with my friend."

Knuckles turning white on the steering wheel, Lucas inhaled sharply. "They all sound awful. I wish I could say no one in Greenhaven is like that, but there are jerks everywhere."

And I'm one of them.

"It just became this whole rumpus in town, so much drama and pettiness. I sold my car and people noticed I was avoiding driving, which just added fuel to the gossip fires. I couldn't stay there."

"So you moved here, where there is just as much drama and pettiness, mostly thanks to me and my family."

He meant it as a joke, and she laughed, which relaxed him.

"Your family is great though. Really."

He took his eyes off the road to steal a quick glance at her to make sure she meant it.

Her eyes were earnest, but then she smirked. "Even if they do have way too many opinions about reality television."

Warmth spread through him.

Even if Juliet said she didn't want to live close to her family, she seemed envious of the relationship Lucas had with his. There was a longing in her, but also a hesitation. He liked that she was open to new people, but kept some things private. He liked that she seemed bolder with him than she did with others. He liked that she wanted to do her own thing but still cared about making her mom proud.

He liked her.

Hopefully when she found out who he was, and why he'd kept this from her for so long, she wouldn't totally hate him.

"So where's this audiobook you promised?"

With a few taps on her phone and his truck's dashboard screen, she had it ready to go. He groaned at how quickly she put it all in place.

"I can't believe you're making me listen to this when I literally finished it less than two weeks ago."

"Books from this time period were meant to be read out loud. It's like Shakespeare. Reading in your head isn't the same."

Grumbling as the pert British accent filled the truck, Lucas soon found himself swept into the story in a way he hadn't been when reading on his own. The miles passed quickly, even with frequent snack stops and pauses in the book for them to discuss what they would have done or said in a character's place.

She shared a little more about her aversion to cars, and it sounded less like a true phobia to overcome and more like a trigger for bad memories. Apparently, his vintage truck was different enough from a "real car" that she wasn't feeling too uncomfortable.

He didn't let that comment slide, laying on a thick layer of what she soon dubbed his "Darcy-esque snobbishness."

Halfway through the book and the drive, Lucas realized he was having fun. Real fun, relaxed, not worrying about who might tease him about it later, or tell his family what they'd seen or overheard. It had been a long time since he'd just been able to be with someone without anyone watching, without comments from at least a dozen people.

It was nice to have something that only belonged to him. The club had felt like that, and the house. It was why he'd been fighting so hard for them. But those things belonged to his family, too, not just him. These moments with Juliet, however, were all his. It was probably why he still couldn't tell her about

Plantsguy95. He didn't like the idea of sharing her with anyone, even with himself.

Well, that makes absolutely no sense. They passed their fifth farm of the trip and Juliet closed her eyes to focus more intently on the audiobook. *You should just tell her.*

The words were right there on the edge of his tongue, but every time he almost said them, he thought of putting her through the rest of the journey with that between them. A repeat of the horrible drive with her ex was the exact opposite of what he wanted this trip to be.

Or, it could be another Audrey situation, and what he'd built up online wouldn't matter to her. Juliet's opinion of Plantsguy95 might not be as high as he assumed. Maybe he'd severely overestimated his importance in her life.

With another hour and six chapters to go, he decided he would tell her after the award ceremony, when they got back to Greenhaven. If she won the prize, then she'd be in a great mood. Even if she were upset, it wouldn't completely ruin her memory of the trip. If she didn't win, it wouldn't make things that much worse.

He'd tell her when they got home.

TWENTY

"Woah, this hotel is gorgeous."

For a random chain hotel in the middle of nowhere suburb of a midwestern city, it was surprising just how nice everything was. Juliet took in the elaborate greenery around the entrance without looking too closely, but Lucas went right up to the planters, investigating each one like it was his job to check for signs of distress.

"This is a very unusual choice for containers."

Unable to hold back her laugh, Juliet put a hand in front of her mouth to at least stifle it. "That's all you have to say about this place? Plants?"

Hurt flashed across his face for a moment, before his signature smirk appeared.

"I mean, it's no Pemberly, but it will do well enough for the evening."

Juliet groaned at his horrible fake British accent. "I did this to myself, didn't I?"

"Shall we inquire as to if a tea tray could be brought to the rooms?"

Shaking her head, she made her way into the lobby to check

in, with Lucas close behind. It was surprising how comfortable she was feeling even after so long in the car together. Even more surprising was how much she wanted to be close to him.

There'd been the physical barrier of the center console between them in the truck, but now he was right there, right behind her. Then he shifted and was standing next to her with his arm brushing against hers. The mossy, outdoor scent of his car had only been somewhat masked by the air freshener he'd hung on the rearview mirror. His truck smelled like him, like leaves and soil, fresh air and sunshine.

It was almost the exact opposite of the new book smell Juliet loved, and yet with his body so close to hers, she found herself leaning in ever so slightly to breathe him in deeply.

"I know, I could totally use a shower after that long in the car." He chuckled, but her cheeks heated to think he'd caught her *sniffing* him.

"You smell great." Her mouth seemed to want to embarrass her even more.

They'd both made their reservations only a few days ago, and the hotel was entirely booked for the editing conference, so their rooms were on completely different floors. It was probably better that way. A nervous energy trembled inside of Juliet to think of him being that close but still so far.

"Are you sure you don't want me to come tonight?" He asked as they made their way to the elevators. Once inside, the small space seemed to fill up with his presence, overpowering her senses. All she could see was his face in the shiny metal walls, and though there was room behind her, he'd chosen to stand right next to her.

Why can't *he come?* Juliet struggled for an answer, though she'd gone through all the reasons logically over the last few days.

The only time The Ex had come to a conference with her,

he'd gone to one session, then spent the rest of the time in their room, complaining about how little there was for him to do. The awards dinner would be especially tedious, the table filled with other editors, all way more experienced and lauded than her. It was the perfect way to highlight just how unimpressive she was.

True, Lucas had just talked with her nonstop for six hours in the car, a large part of that time about books. There was no indication he'd found that tedious or Juliet uninteresting.

But she didn't want to push her luck.

There was no way to tell him all of this, of course, so she settled on something close to the truth. "It'll be super boring. You'll have more fun watching movies and hanging out at the pool."

"Who'll take your picture when you win?"

Her heart gave an uneven thump. The blind confidence in her abilities he'd never seen firsthand was adorable. "*If* I win, there's a photographer."

The elevator dinged and opened to her floor. Turning to give him a smile, he put his arm across the doors so they wouldn't shut on her.

"Whatever happens, feel free to call me after, okay? I'll just be a few floors away."

Her heart gave a loud thump against her chest. The doors closed slowly on his earnest, smiling face.

She stood there for close to a minute before she shook herself out of her Lucas-induced haze and made her way down the hallway to her room. It was just as impressive as the rest of the hotel.

Once she hung her dress in the closet and placed her tiny bag of toiletries in the bathroom, she lay back on her bed and opened up her phone. Nervous scrolling for a few hours was exactly what she needed.

Plantsguy95 had been quiet for a few days, but then again,

so had she. Most of her messages had been back and forth with Charlotte, trying to figure out what she should wear to the event. She hadn't mentioned Lucas driving her, since Charlotte didn't know about Juliet's issue with cars, but they'd talked about a lot of other things they hadn't before in the last few days. How nervous she was about the awards, how frustrated she was with her family not showing support, how lonely she still felt in Greenhaven sometimes. It was like calling Charlotte on the night of the kiss with Lucas had broken down some sort of barrier.

It was nice, having someone to share more of her life with, now that there was actually something to tell.

Not that there was much to tell about Lucas yet. He had driven her, had taken a separate hotel room, and promised he'd stay there until the event was over. She was nervous enough as it was, she didn't need him staring at her from the audience. If she lost, she didn't want him to see her cry in public, or try to soothe her. If she won, it felt like too soon in their relationship to do a big hug and kiss thing.

Relationship. Was that what they had?

Then what did she have with Plantsguy95? Her finger hovered over his leafy profile picture. He was a friend, just like Charlotte. Well, not quite like Charlotte, who she'd met in person. Sadness sank into her chest when she realized she might never meet this mystery plant guru face to face. Unless she took the initiative and asked him to meet. Which she wouldn't do, because of Lucas, right?

There was a knock at her door.

Expecting Lucas, she hastily stowed her phone in her purse and smoothed down her hair before opening the door.

Her mouth dropped open.

"Surprise!" Charlotte threw her arms around Juliet and squeezed.

"What are you doing here?" She stepped aside to let Charlotte into the room.

"You sounded so nervous about this, and I remember how hard the last conference was for you, so I wanted to be here to support you."

"But you had that alumni football event with your husband, at your college."

Charlotte waved a hand. "We do that every year and I haven't seen you in two years."

Tears sprang to Juliet's eyes and she blinked them away. Even if she made it sound like it wasn't a big deal, Charlotte had given up an important weekend to help Juliet. No one had ever made such an effort for her. Except maybe Lucas who had driven her.

"Thank you." The words came out a little gruff, so she softened them with a smile. "Did you get a room?"

"I can see if they have one, but would you mind a sleepover? I'll take the couch."

Maybe it was the long drive being such a success, but Juliet found herself excited about the idea of a sleepover with a friend. Her first in decades, not that she'd had that many as a teenager.

"Did you drive here? On your own?"

"Not exactly." Juliet sat down on the bed and Charlotte took the armchair facing it. "Lucas drove me."

"The kiss from last week?" She wiggled excitedly in the chair. "You never gave me details, by the way. Just a quick note that everything was fine."

At her simple request for details, everything inside Juliet seized up. While she didn't think Charlotte would use anything against her, sharing face to face was different from messages or over the phone. The barrier of technology kept a layer between Juliet and those hard, scary feelings of betrayal she'd pushed away for so long.

"It was—is—fine." Juliet picked at some invisible lint on her shirt. "And now he drove me here."

"He's staying here?" She raised her eyebrows and looked around the room.

"No, he has his own room."

"I can't wait to meet him tonight."

"I asked him not to come."

"What? Why not?" Charlotte stuck out her lower lip.

"He's not my boyfriend. He's just a friend, who drove me here." Okay, now that she was saying it out loud, it sounded ridiculous to not have him come to dinner tonight.

Charlotte seemed to agree, even though she was shaking her head. "He drove you all the way here and he's just going to spend the night in his room watching a movie while you drink free champagne and eat duck?"

"I don't want him to see me if I lose."

There, that was the truth without too many details. The hitch in her voice seemed to let Charlotte know that Juliet was at her limit of sharing, since she didn't push and merely nodded slowly.

"Okay, so then it'll just be us. Win or lose, I'll be your buffer."

"Thanks."

They exchanged smiles, an apologetic one from Juliet and a warm one from Charlotte, who clapped her hands eagerly.

"Now, let's see that dress I convinced you to wear."

Fifteen minutes later, Juliet had slipped into the deep-purple, cocktail-length dress that was a perfect mix of comfortable and flattering. Flaring out at the hips, the A-line silhouette was classic in a way that felt true to Juliet's day-to-day style. It didn't feel like she was in a costume the way she normally did in fancy dresses.

"Oh, Juliet, you look great!"

"It has pockets."

Charlotte chuckled and rolled her eyes. "I said you looked great, not the dress. It's very nice though. Good to know about the pockets."

Heat flooded Juliet's cheeks. "You look amazing."

Charlotte's pink, floaty, frothy dress was the perfect sartorial match to her personality. It was also bright enough for most eyes to be on her, not Juliet, which was more than all right with Juliet. "Thanks." Charlotte beamed and checked her watch. "Ready to go? Cocktail hour is starting soon."

There was a flutter in her stomach as she nodded. She wasn't sure if it was the idea of winning, losing, or just being around so many people that made her most nervous.

"You should still go by Lucas's room before we go down, so he can wish you luck. Thank him for driving you."

Without thinking too hard, she nodded again. The walk would help with her jittery nerves.

The ride up to the seventh floor was quick, but the hallway to his room felt like it was miles long. All the reasons she'd had for not having him come with her now seemed silly. Was it too late to ask him to come? He probably didn't have any nice clothes with him.

When he answered the door, he was wearing almost no clothes.

"Well, hello there, abs." Charlotte's words weren't quite a whisper, and based on Lucas's giant grin, he must have heard them.

"Hi." He leaned against the doorframe, arms crossed over a shirtless chest. All he had on were swimming trunks. "You look beautiful, Juliet."

Words were getting stuck in her throat, but she did manage a smile. Which might have been more of a grimace. A few more moments ticked by without her brain being able to form and produce words.

Finally, Charlotte nudged her from behind. "Say thank you, Juliet."

"Thank you, Juliet."

Oh, sweet oxford comma. That was worse than being speechless. Every part of her body was on fire from the combination of embarrassment and pure attraction.

To his credit, Lucas didn't laugh, though his grin did widen a little, taking on a slightly more devilish quality.

"If I'd have known this was all it took to distract you, I'd have cleaned out Maude's house this way."

The teasing snapped her out of it. Just like the first time they'd met, she didn't hesitate, didn't filter the first sassy words that sprang from her mouth. "All that would have done is get sweat all over those old cable bills from the eighties you insisted were priceless journals."

She tossed her head and heard Charlotte snicker behind her. "I just wanted to let you know you don't have to worry about the pictures. Charlotte ended up coming."

"Nice to meet you, Charlotte." His eyes focused on her friend. "Be sure to take one of her face when she wins."

"You've never even read anything I've edited."

"I've seen how you sort through books and documents that don't belong to you. I know you take care of things. If that's what the award is for, then it's yours."

Rendered speechless again, Juliet took a step back and bumped into Charlotte, who put a hand on her arm to steady her.

"That's so sweet, Lucas. I'll take lots of pictures, don't

worry." She looked at her watch. "We don't want to be late. Enjoy your evening at the pool."

Her hand squeezed Juliet's arm and she turned away, following Charlotte down the hallway. The jittery nerves were worse than ever, but they had less to do with the upcoming event and more to do with wanting to ditch the dress and join Lucas at the pool.

The indecision must have shown in her face, because once they were in the elevator heading down, Charlotte chuckled and shook her head. "Don't worry, you can meet up with him afterward."

Juliet fiddled with the strap on her purse that contained only her room key and phone. "I wouldn't want to bother him. He's already done enough."

"I don't think you'd bother him at all. I've seen that look on a man's face before. He likes you Juliet. A lot. Even before he saw you in that dress."

Now completely unsettled and every nerve jangling, they walked into a room full of strangers. Juliet took a deep breath and plastered on a smile, just as Charlotte gave her arm a squeeze. At least she had a friend by her side.

TWENTY-ONE

"I can't wait to show Lucas the picture of your face." Slightly drunk, a beaming Charlotte yelled into Juliet's ear.

Clutching the chunk of glass in the shape of a star etched with her name on it, Juliet leaned back against the elevator wall and laughed.

"Not the first one. I have a piece of food in my mouth."

"I don't think that'll change how he feels."

"No sense risking it." She pushed the button for the third floor. "In fact, let me just stop and brush my teeth really quickly."

"Fresh breath is essential for whatever happens next." Charlotte giggled and gave Juliet a saucy wink and elbow nudge. While they'd both had a drink during cocktail hour, Charlotte had continued drinking during dinner, which had lasted way longer than expected. Juliet had been too nervous to have anything other than water with her meal, and she was grateful she'd been mostly clearheaded to accept the award. Though a bit of fuzziness would have been nice right now, so she didn't overthink what she would say to Lucas when she showed up at his hotel room door at eleven o'clock at night.

"He might already be asleep. It was a long drive."

"He won't be. He wants to know how it went."

"Well, he can wait until I've brushed my teeth then."

They walked into their hotel room to find flowers sitting on the table with a note.

Whatever happened, you deserve these.

"Oh, that's too sweet." Charlotte leaned down and inhaled the red and orange lilies.

Juliet's skin tingled, her head swimming as the thick scent of lilies engulfed her. This was too much, too fast. She liked him, of course she liked him, she'd known that for a while now. If she were being totally honest with herself, she wasn't sure she'd ever truly disliked him.

Toothbrush in one hand, she reached for her phone with the other. Whenever the world was too much, turning off her brain with some mindless scrolling was the only remedy.

With a stab of guilt in her chest, she realized there was someone else she should tell about her big win too. Plantsguy95 hadn't been in her thoughts that much all evening, they'd been so filled with the award . . . and Lucas.

It was funny how, in such a short time, the feelings she'd had about an online friend had dissipated. She felt a little ridiculous to think about whatever inklings she'd had for Plantsguy95, now that she had Lucas saying sweet things and sending her flowers. Even if Plantsguy95 had been absent the last week, she was sure he'd want to know that she'd won.

There were no new messages from Plantsguy95, but he had posted a new photo, which she tried not to read too much into. It could dave been scheduled in advance, the way she did.

It was an interesting shot of a huge variegated Monstera plant, its holey leaves a speckled white and pink. It was rare, and Plantsguy95 was so excited about it, he misspelled a few words and had made some interesting punctuation choices. She was so focused on his sloppy copy, it took her a full minute to notice the mirror behind the plant had an embossed logo with a name underneath.

The name of this hotel.

A pit opened up in her stomach. She looked again, taking in every detail of the photo, just to be sure she wasn't imagining things.

When Charlotte knocked on the door to the bathroom, the look on Juliet's face must have been something terrible, because she sat down right away next to her.

"What's wrong? Is your family okay?"

Holding out her phone with a trembling hand, Juliet shook her head. "Do those look familiar to you?"

Charlotte leaned over and frowned. "Aren't those the weird plants downstairs? Did you post this? Not really on brand."

"Plantsguy95 posted it."

The gasp that Charlotte gave was reality TV dramatic, but Juliet was freaking out too much to truly appreciate it.

"He's here?"

"I think he's Lucas."

"The guy from your town?" Charlotte's voice was reaching an unnatural pitch.

"It would just be too much of a coincidence."

"He must not realize who you are." Charlotte's eyes lit up. "You have to tell him. Though, honestly, if he didn't make the connection between JCEdits and driving Juliet Chapman to an editing awards ceremony, I'm not sure I want you canoodling with such a cretin."

That wasn't it, though. His post had been too unplanned, too enthusiastic about the rare plant. Besides, Lucas was straightforward enough to tell her something like that outright, he wouldn't try to do it in some cutesy way.

Scrolling through her messages, she looked at the date of the last one from Plantsguy95. It was the night of the art show. Is that when he'd realized it? Maybe Charlotte was right and he was trying to tell her something with the photo.

No, some instinct in her churning stomach told her it wasn't that simple. The part of her that had been deeply hurt, the part that didn't trust easily and that had learned to be wary when something felt too good to be true, told her he'd known much longer.

Pride and Prejudice. He'd been reading it weeks ago. And she'd been bugging Plantsguy95 about it for even longer.

There was only one reason he wouldn't have said anything to her as soon as he realized who she was. He was trying to manipulate her. It was The Ex, and her former best friend, all over again. Someone she trusted, using what she said against her.

Juliet had been worried about telling Charlotte too much, but this whole time she'd been giving endless fodder to someone hell-bent on bringing down an organization she loved. One of the only places in town she felt like herself, like she belonged.

The only other place she'd felt like that recently was with Lucas's cousins.

Bile rose in her throat. Had they known this whole time? Was the entire Geis family set against her?

She looked again at his account, and the photo was no longer there.

"Looks like he deleted it." Charlotte was looking down at her own phone with a frown on her face.

That wasn't a good sign. Still, a tiny part of her hoped it wasn't true. There was one way to find out for sure.

She swiped to her phonebook and tapped on a name.

"Hey, Juliet, everything okay? It's kind of late." Mari's warm voice came through, then turned serious. "Is Lucas okay?"

"Um, yeah, he's fine." Juliet felt ridiculous, but at Charlotte's urging gestures, she said, "Sorry about the late call. It's just, um, does Lucas have a social media account about plants?"

There was the smallest pause on the other end of the line, and that told Juliet everything she needed to know. The tears came quickly, and she blinked them away. The blood rushed through her ears, so it was hard to hear when Mari finally spoke. The first word was a swear.

"We should have made him tell you sooner."

"We?" The word was warbly with unshed tears.

"I'm so sorry, Juliet, it was such a ridiculous idea looking back. I can't believe he convinced us it would work. But he really wanted to save Maude's house and—"

"Thank you for being honest." Juliet tapped to end the call and sunk down onto the bathroom floor, dissolving into sobs.

Yet again she'd been played for a fool. A secret people were laughing over while she was cluelessly going about her life, thinking things were good. Great, even.

The gossip, the secrets, all of it was supposed to be in the past. Greenhaven was supposed to be a new start for her, one without all the small town drama that had ruined her life before. And yet all because of some stupid house that neither she nor Lucas had any control over, he'd decided it was a good idea to trick her, to lie to her for weeks. To make her vulnerable again, to hope again, only for her heart to be ripped out just as she thought something good would happen.

Charlotte curled around her, folding Juliet into her arms as she cried.

The tears didn't actually last that long, but even before they'd stopped, she'd already started speaking. The story of her ex, her best friend who'd used her to get to him, the horrible car ride, everything. She'd been holding back from Charlotte for years, and while there was still the potential she could hurt Juliet with all of this, she was too miserable to worry about that right now. What she needed was exactly what Charlotte was giving her: quiet acceptance and gentle strokes down her back as Juliet hiccupped away the last of her tears.

It wasn't until she tried to stand that Charlotte finally spoke. "Don't you dare move. I'll take care of everything, don't worry."

SAGE

What are you doing in Springfield?

After ignoring the texts from his cousins for the entire day, Lucas decided it was finally time to answer a few. The first batch from this morning were all about the new space and plans for their first meeting there next week. He knew they were expecting a firestorm of riled up responses from him, but all the energy he'd been focusing on that was now wrapped up in the looming confession to Juliet. Even after dozens of laps in the pool, his mind was empty of ideas on how to not screw it up.

While he was scrolling through his messages, deciding who to answer first, a new one from Sage popped up.

LUCAS

How do you know I'm in Springfield?

SAGE

Your most recent post. The Monstera is stunning, and that's a very fancy hotel.

You really went all out to impress Juliet, huh?

Lucas looked in horror at the image on his screen. He'd taken the picture so quickly, he'd been so excited, that he'd totally missed how prominent the hotel's logo was in the mirror the plant was in front of. The logo included not just the name of the hotel, but the city.

Fear building in his chest, he checked to see who'd already viewed the post. Dread dropped like a bomb in his belly. Juliet had seen it.

He deleted the post and started hyperventilating. Then he started pacing around the room, but doing that at the same time, he was struggling to breathe just wore him out. He collapsed onto the bed and stared up at the ceiling, panic coursing through his veins, unable to do anything about it.

After allowing himself several minutes of anxious panic, he took a deep breath and tried to sort things out. Just seeing the photo didn't mean she'd realized who he was. She could have just clicked past it, not taken in all the details. He hadn't even noticed the logo when he'd posted it, so she probably hadn't either.

Suffering succulents, there was no way he was that lucky. He'd been playing his luck for weeks. He should have told her ages ago, but now here he was, in a mess of his own making.

At least Sage didn't know why he was really here or she'd have wasted no time in rubbing "I told you so" in his face. It was a small silver lining—extremely small—but he would take what he could get right now.

His phone dinged, and he looked down to see a message from Mari.

MARI

You're an idiot.

The blood in his body froze. Juliet knew. Before he could even think of how to face her, to prepare the words he could say to make this okay, there was a knock at the door.

Flinging it open, he was already apologizing. "Juliet, I'm so sorry, I—"

"She's not here." It was Charlotte, her friend, looking absolutely murderous. "I just wanted to let you know that I'll be driving her home tomorrow. Not that you would have worried."

"Of course I'd worry, I care about her so much. I . . . " He took a deep breath, his hands gripping the edge of the doorway. "I'm falling for her. That's why I was going to tell her when we got home. I swear. I hated that this was still a secret."

Charlotte looked him up and down, taking in his rumpled hair and threadbare shirt. It was probably a good thing he hadn't been down there with them. Even in his nicest clothes, he wasn't anywhere near as fancy as Juliet and her professional friends. Audrey had always told him just how much he was lacking. Juliet would never even think that about someone.

And now he'd probably lost her forever.

"Can you just tell her one thing for me?"

"Depends what it is." She gave him a glare to rival the Geis women.

"Just tell her I never meant to hurt her. I just wanted her to see the garden club in a better light. To see how much the house meant to us."

"You didn't think she'd figure that out on her own?" Charlotte shook her head and sighed. "All abs and floppy hair and no brain. Just like her ex."

Ouch. The comparison hurt, but he'd been lying to her, just like the jerk who'd dumped her in her car had been.

"I'm sorry. Please tell her that."

Pursing her lips, Charlotte tilted her head, the light from the hallway sparkling in her earrings. "I will if you tell me one thing."

"Anything."

"What does the 95 mean?"

"What?"

For the first time, Charlotte looked hesitant. "In your username. I thought it was for a birth year, and this guy she was chatting with online was only in his twenties."

Pain ripped through his chest. Juliet had tried to figure out who Plantsguy95 was. She'd talked about him with her closest friend. If he'd told her as soon as he'd realized who she was, it might have been awkward, but it probably would have ended well. Not like tonight.

"It's my house number."

Charlotte raised an eyebrow. "How long have you lived there?"

He shrugged. "My whole life."

At her wry smile, he flushed. It was the truth, but somehow felt like it was the wrong answer.

"Interesting. You identify more with your house than your birthday."

With that cryptic remark, she turned and walked away, back to Juliet to repair the damage Lucas had caused.

TWENTY-TWO

At the Friends of the Library's annual books and beer-tasting event, Juliet tried to hide in the back near the food tables. It was on the Cork side of Cork and Beans, and while most of the faces were familiar, Juliet barely registered any of them.

It had been only three days since the long, quiet drive home with Charlotte from the editing conference. There was no way she'd ever be able to pay Charlotte back for the rental car, but Charlotte said she'd write it off as a business expense. She'd even offered to stay a few days, but Juliet had already taken up enough of her time. Charlotte had a life to get back to, a husband.

Now Juliet wished she'd asked her to stay, if only to be her buffer again. Juliet didn't really feel up to seeing people, but she'd agreed to help with this event months ago, and wasn't going to let Denise down. It wasn't her fault Juliet had gotten her heart broken.

It was funny to think that if she'd just refused to help clear out the Periwinkle Mansion all those weeks ago, then none of this would have happened.

As Juliet gave a weak smile to the stream of people walking

past the table with their stack of used books for sale, many that she recognized by face if not by name from around town, she realized the situation with Lucas had been inevitable. Greenhaven was big, but not that big. Eventually, one or the other would have either mentioned their town in their online exchanges or posted something familiar the other recognized. How would she have felt to discover Plantsguy95 was Lucas if she'd never gotten to know Lucas first?

That kind of thinking was pointless though. With a stab of pain in her chest, she flicked through one of the two copies of *Pride and Prejudice* they had for sale that evening. She had gotten to know Lucas, to like him even—more than her bruised heart was willing to admit right now—and instead of excitement to discover an online crush was local, she was horrified at the deception.

She put down the Austen and ran her hands over the spines of the books laid out on long tables against the back wall. Juliet inhaled, trying to calm herself with that old-book smell. Instead, her stomach turned at the moist, yeasty odor of beer that permeated the air. Well, it was a bar, after all. The combination coffee shop and brewery was usually one of her favorite places, with its sunny courtyard separating the two spaces, but tonight Juliet was counting the minutes until she could leave.

Someone cleared their throat and Juliet turned with a half-hearted "Can I help you?"

"Juliet, hi."

It was Mari. Unsure what to say, Juliet's entire body tensed. She felt just as betrayed by the Geis cousins as by Lucas. More, in a way, since to have all eight of them in on the secret and not give anything away truly spoke to how much on the outside Juliet was with them.

Shoulders scrunched up against her ears, she turned away, but not before noticing the tall, handsome man standing behind

Mari, looking at her like a man in the desert looked at a glass of water. Juliet's stomach sank. They must have been out for drinks, like a regular couple, when she'd seen Juliet and the books.

"Look, I'm really sorry." Mari stepped around the table to face Juliet. "We all are."

Still not looking at Mari, Juliet bit her lip to keep from crying, but her voice was still trembling. "I kind of expect men to be jerks at this point, but you all seemed like my f-friends."

To her credit, she didn't even glance at her boyfriend, or try to say some men weren't that bad. "We are your friends, and we are one hundred percent on your side in this."

She very much doubted that. "But he's your family."

"And he was a total idiot. We all were, to have gone along with his ridiculous idea, but none of us thought it would hurt anybody. That was never our intent. You have to believe that."

She believed that the Geis woman had believed it was possible. It still didn't change the fact that someone *had* gotten hurt.

Luckily, Denise came up and saved her from having to respond.

"Juliet, there you are. I wanted to congratulate you in person for your award." The older woman reached out, and Juliet found herself encased in a hug. It was a short one that left her feeling confused, but oddly warmed.

"What award?" Mari asked, turning her warm and open face to Denise, whose entire demeanor shifted.

Flush and hang. A meeting of the extroverts. Juliet would have laughed if she weren't so miserable.

"Juliet's a freelance editor, and the work she did on the library's latest literary magazine won an award with the country's biggest editing association."

Now the warmth spread to Juliet's cheeks, face, neck, everywhere, as Mari's eyes lit up. "That's wonderful."

"My grandfather started the magazine when he founded the Friends and actually had a lot of help from—"

Someone called to Denise, and she rushed off with an apology.

The crowded bar buzzed with conversations, and Juliet inhaled the tangy beer smell of it deep into her lungs. Mari cleared her throat. "It sounds like a big deal. You must be really proud."

"You hadn't heard already?"

Mari shook her head. "Lucas didn't tell us where you were last week."

For some reason, that warmed Juliet most of all. There was no question he'd gone to his cousins for help. He could have told them everything, where they went, why he'd driven her so far, and yet he'd kept this from them, as promised.

"Why didn't you post about it on social media? That's so exciting."

"You follow me?"

"Um, we all do." Now Mari looked embarrassed. She took a book in her hands—the same *Pride and Prejudice* copy Juliet had been perusing earlier—and fanned through the pages. "Ever since he started talking about this online friend nonstop over the winter."

"But you didn't know who I was back then."

She shrugged and closed the book, but held onto it. "A follow is an easy way to support. It was someone who was clearly important to him, so we all did it."

Tears sprang to her eyes to think of how very close and loyal the Geis family was. Her own mother and sister didn't follow her account. It was why she hadn't bothered to post yet.

Well, that, and she had been in a depressed funk since Charlotte had dropped her off.

"It's not that big of a deal. It's not like the award means anything if you're not an editor."

"It means something to you. You should celebrate."

Juliet gestured around the bar. "This is about as wild as I get. Books and beer."

"We could buy you a drink." Mari's eyes flicked to her boyfriend and her lips curved up automatically.

"I probably shouldn't. Gotta keep an eye on the cash box."

Drinks with a swoony couple wasn't exactly her idea of an enjoyable evening.

Mari shifted on her feet. "You could always come to *Bachelor* night this week? We could celebrate then."

The hesitation must have shown on Juliet's face.

"We won't talk about Lucas, or any guys," said Mari. "I promise. *Bachelor* night is about one thing only."

Juliet smiled at that. They were very serious about their rule.

"We really like having you there. But we also understand if you don't want anything to do with the Geis family for a while."

"I'll think about it."

That was the best she could do and Mari seemed to understand that. With a final smile, she stuffed some bills into the donation jar and left with her boyfriend and the copy of *Pride and Prejudice* she'd been leafing through.

In the end, Juliet did have a drink, but by herself, with a book keeping her company in a quiet corner booth of the bar. Her conversation with Mari from earlier was still on her mind, and now she was in that weird mood where she didn't want to talk to people, but she didn't want to be alone in her apartment. Reading in a bar was the ideal solution.

Until Stephen appeared at her booth with a beer in hand and a stern expression.

"May I join you?"

Juliet blinked up at him. "Um, sure."

He sat—slowly, she noticed—and took a gulp from his glass before putting it down on the table. "Plant people are interesting."

"Sorry?"

"I saw one of the Geis women talking to you earlier."

When Juliet frowned in confusion, he continued.

"My husband used to be in the garden club."

"I didn't know that."

"Why would you? I never told you."

Fair point. So much of Juliet's life was spent feeling guilty or anxious about not knowing something she shouldn't be expected to. Yet that didn't stop the tears or racing pulse when the situation arose. Having Stephen let her off the hook was like a weight lifting from her shoulders.

She took a sip from her drink so any redness in her face could be attributed to the alcohol.

"When I got too sick to work, he didn't have much time to be an active member, then he discovered pickleball and that's all he does these days." Stephen leaned back in the booth and crossed his arms. "We still have about eight hundred plants in the house though."

This was more than Juliet had anticipated hearing from Stephen when he sat down, and she had no idea why he was sharing so much. "You met him at a pie-eating contest, right?"

"That's the story we tell people. Honestly, we met online."

This wasn't what Juliet had expected him to say. "But you had that whole conversation with my mom." Her chest tightened. How many more liars were there in this town?

"Technically, we did meet there, for the first time, in

person." He leaned forward and dropped his voice. "A few months before, we'd met in a chat room."

Juliet almost laughed at his whispered admission. "I remember those. The early days of the internet were wild. My mom had really strict rules for me and my sister." The slow evolution from being wary of strangers on the internet to her entire life being online wasn't unique to Juliet, but she was in that odd generation who had spent most of her childhood without a computer. Another difference between her and most of the people she interacted with who were either young high school volunteers for the Friends, or in their late middle age like Denise and Stephen.

Lucas was in that same in-between generation, too, but she wasn't thinking about him right now.

"So you understand why we don't tell people above a certain age that's how we met."

Juliet nodded. "What about if you met someone online but then met them in person and they didn't tell you who they really were for weeks?"

"I feel like there is more to the story."

Juliet pursed her lips then brought her drink to her mouth.

He also took a sip, and his eyes lingered on hers above the rims of their glasses. "Without knowing more, all I can say is that as you get older, the details around how you met someone matter less, and how they treat you when you're together matter more."

"Well, he was lying to me the whole time we were together."

"I think he was lying to himself most of all."

Juliet had thought the same thing more than once but wasn't ready to say that out loud.

"That applies to friends as well."

This obviously was a reference to Mari.

Suddenly, Juliet was all peopled out for the evening. With a bang, she set her empty glass onto the table. "I need to head home."

Fearing that saying anything more would make the tears that had been building all night finally fall, she left without a backward glance at Stephen, or even saying goodbye.

TWENTY-THREE

"You are the world's biggest nincompoop."

With his head buried in his hands, Lucas couldn't see which of his cousins said that, but his guess was Violet.

His quietest cousin didn't say much, but when she did, each word landed like a punch.

"I realize that. Do any of you have a suggestion about what to do?"

"Have you tried calling her or sending her a message?" That sounded like Mari.

"It's been almost a week, what do you think? Do I look like an idiot?"

He peeked through his hands to the disappointed glares of all eight Geis women that all practically screamed "absolutely."

They'd all been ignoring his calls and messages all week. When he stopped by one of their houses, they all claimed to be busy. It was like they'd taken a vote to give him the cold shoulder on behalf of Juliet. After all his griping lately that they were too involved in his life, it was an ironic punishment for them to shut him out like that.

Not sure what else to do, he'd shown up at Bachelor night

with an enormous box of chocolates and a bottle of wine that Kirk at the liquor store had promised was the best, even if it wasn't the most expensive. While Lucas, of course, wanted to patch things up with his cousins, there was a small part of him who'd hoped Juliet might be there like she had for the last few weeks.

Of course she wasn't there, because of course she would be mad at his cousins as well. After all, they'd known about this, though Lucas took full responsibility. He'd never actually needed their approval, only their promise to not tell her, which they'd kept out of family loyalty to him. The same family loyalty Juliet had praised on their road trip was now the reason she was mad at her only friends in town.

At least that same family loyalty was finally giving him much-needed advice after staying silent through the entire show while they tore through the chocolate. Sage hid the wine away "for a more festive occasion."

Their advice, however, was less than helpful.

"I sent tons of messages. They're all left on read but no answer. She doesn't want to talk to me."

"So don't talk to her for a while." Heather shrugged, like it was the most obvious answer in the world. "Give her time."

"I can't just do nothing." There was a problem, and he would fix it. That's what he did with the people he cared about, no matter who had actually caused the problem. Though in this case there was no doubt he was the reason for Juliet's pain.

"For once in your life, your stubbornness won't help." Mari chuckled. "Actually, I can't think of a time it did help . . ."

"There was that dangerous outbuilding behind the grocery store kids were using to deal drugs."

Sage waved a hand. "They were going to tear it down anyway."

"The plaque for war veterans in town square."

"The Mayor only did that to get re-elected." Mari popped another chocolate into her mouth.

"The football boycott for Sage when Antonio dumped her."

"The school lost a ton of funding for that, and the principal was pissed," said Violet.

Throwing up his hands, he stood. "Fine, nothing I do ever makes a difference, does it?"

At his fierce expression, they all clammed up and let him rant.

"Nothing I do is good enough. I give everything I have to those I care about, and it doesn't make a difference. You all don't understand the pressure I have on me to protect everyone. No one else will do it if I don't. You still have Aunt Louise and Uncle Henry, and who do I have?

"Then the one time I try to do something on my own, to improve things for myself for once, and first it lost me a girl-friend, who, fine, wasn't that great, but she was still someone I loved once upon a time. And now the same stupid account has lost me someone else I—"

He stopped and ran his hands through his hair. If he was going to say the words, they wouldn't be to his cousins first.

"I'd close the account if it weren't for all the people I'm helping. Friends I've made there, people who come to me for advice. Between that, and this family, the club, this town . . . I'm just messing everything up. What else do you want from me?"

He fell to the floor, missing the couch completely.

Arms circled him from both sides, and someone else ran their fingers through his hair. That must have been Lily massaging his scalp. It reminded him that it had been ages since he'd been in for a haircut, but he'd been putting it off ever since he noticed how Juliet always stared when he ran his hands through his hair.

"We don't want anything, dummy."

"We just want you to be happy."

"Just be yourself. That's enough."

"Let one of us help run the account if you need a break. We didn't know it was stressing you out that much."

"We can help more with the club too. Nobody said you had to do it all."

"Yeah, that new meeting room is super boring. And what's with the no plants rule in the building? I'll totally call Mayor Taylor to complain, don't worry."

For the next few minutes, he let himself be hugged and loved by his family, by the people who had known him all his life, and who were still there even when he messed up.

Even in the middle of all this love from his family, his thoughts turned to Juliet. He wondered who she'd been able to talk to about all this, who she had as her support network. A week ago, he would have been there, either in person or online.

That's what he hated himself most for. Not that the lies weren't bad, but when his whole life was about helping people, about being there for them, to know Juliet had one less person in her corner because of him felt like the worst thing he could have done to her.

"Have you told Juliet about any of this?" Sage's voice drifted over the rest, and for a moment, he thought his cousin had actually read his mind for real this time. "About all this pressure you feel? About Audrey? About your parents?"

His silence gave her the answer she needed. She sighed. "Oh, Lucas. Why do you hide so much?"

"I don't hide anything from you. I told you all about my idiotic plan."

"I'm not talking about hiding things from us." She shook her head.

"Oh."

As if to make sure he fully understood what Sage had

meant, Mari spoke up from somewhere in the middle of the cluster of cousins surrounding him.

"I feel like you replaced getting to know you with getting to know the family," Mari said, her eyes meeting his across the top of several heads of dark hair.

"What do you mean?"

He should probably get up off the floor, but it was much too comfortable having them all squashed in around him. Like physical proof they would always be there for him.

"Just because we know everything about you, and we're hanging out with someone you like, doesn't mean that person will get to know you any better." She paused and looked thoughtful for a moment. "Well, they will in a way, but really all it will do is just confirm whatever they were feeling about you before."

His confusion must have shown on his face and she let out a sigh. The others rolled their eyes at his denseness.

"If it had been all of you stuck in that elevator with my boyfriend"—her eyes shone the way they always did whenever she talked about him—"he'd have gotten to know me, sure, and probably agreed to go out with me. But I don't think he would have fallen the way he did. I did that on my own, by sharing everything myself, even though it was the scariest thing I'd ever done. Get it?"

"Not really."

Except, in the deepest part of him, Lucas knew exactly what she meant and what he had to do. That didn't mean it would be any easier to actually do it.

From the depths of her blanket nest, Juliet heard the doorbell ring. She released a quiet groan, then, deciding it didn't matter if whoever was at the door heard just how miserable she was, she groaned louder.

The doorbell rang again.

With a curse, she dragged herself out of bed and down the hallway to the front door. It was a short hallway, but today, stuffy and congested with the cold to end all colds, it felt like a marathon.

Thinking of marathons made her think of Tony, her brother-in-law, which made her think of her sister, which made her think of her mother.

"Mom?" she asked when she got to the intercom next to her door.

"No." It was a man's voice. Juliet sighed. Her mom had probably sent food again.

Now she'd have to call her to thank her and Juliet was too tired today. Plus she wasn't even that hungry. "You can leave it out there, thanks." One of her neighbors would either scoop it up for themselves or throw it out once it had been there for longer than a day.

"Juliet, can I come up, please?"

Her stomach dropped. Already queasy from her cold, she put a hand against the wall to steady herself. "Lucas?"

"I just want to talk."

"I don't think that's a good idea. I'm really sick."

There was no answer but she heard footsteps in the stairwell. A neighbor coming into the building must have let him in. She supposed she deserved that kind of karma for letting so much food go to waste in the vestibule.

Panic simmering in her stomach, she looked around her apartment. It was in complete chaos, worse than even what happened during one of her editing sprints. She'd been sick for the better part of a week. Empty tissue boxes were on every available surface, and while most of the tissues had made it into the trash, there were many still shoved into the mugs that dotted the living room furniture like mushrooms sprouting after rain. The pile of books next to the couch was so high it threatened to tip over. Just as she rushed over to start tidying them away, they *did* tip over—with a spectacular crash. Of course, that was when Lucas knocked on her door.

"Just a minute," she called, and hurried to pile everything onto a chair and cover it with a blanket. It wasn't great, but it was slightly better than before. Now it looked like she'd only been sick for a day or two, and just needed to vacuum to get things back in order.

Finally, she grabbed the first coat she put her hands on in her hall closet and slipped it over her book-print pajamas. They were the furthest thing from revealing, but they were more than a little embarrassing. When she was sick, she needed comfort, and books did that for her whether she was reading them or wearing them.

When she opened the door, Lucas was standing there, a potted plant in one hand, a Tupperware in the other. "Hi."

"Hello." She sniffed, but instead of sounding indignant, she sounded just as sick as she was. "What are you doing here?"

"Can I come in?"

"I'm sick."

"I know. That's why I'm here."

That surprised her enough that she stepped away from the door and let him into her apartment.

As he turned slowly to take in the small space, she realized it was the first time he'd ever been here. What must he be thinking? Was he seeing all the tissues that had escaped their mugs, or judging the books still on the floor?

Then she remembered she didn't care, because he was a lying jerk face who cared more about some stupid house than he did about her.

"I'd offer you something to drink but I don't want to." Also, she didn't have anything, but she wasn't about to admit that.

"I deserve that." He held out the plant and the Tupperware. "These are for you."

Figuring the sooner he delivered things the sooner he'd be gone, she took them, and set them on the table in front of the couch. She noticed the cookies in the Tupperware were gingersnaps, her favorite. It could have been chance, but there'd been a long discussion during their car trip about the kinds of tea and biscuits Jane Austen ate. The thought softened her the tiniest bit, until she remembered with a sinking feeling that cookies were also something she'd chatted about with Plantsguy95.

"How did you know I was sick?"

"You didn't come to *Bachelor* night this week."

"One of your cousins told you?" A shiver of the doubt that had mostly calmed over the last few weeks rose to the surface again. *Bachelor* night last week had been a test, in a way. As Mari had promised, there was no talk of Lucas, only the show.

But they'd never promised to not talk to him about her.

"They weren't gossiping. They only told me because I asked like five hundred times and I finally wore them down."

The corner of his lips twitched and Juliet squashed the urge to do the same.

"Why were you asking about me?"

Instead of answering, he simply looked at her, eyes deep and warm, the intensity higher than she'd ever seen it.

"Oh."

There was an awkward silence that stretched for way too long. It was his turn to say something, but he didn't seem to know that.

"Thank you for the cookies," she said, tucking her hands into the sleeves of her coat.

"They're gingersnaps."

"My favorite."

"I know. You told me on the drive."

Her heart wanted to believe that was the only way he knew, but her head told her to stay wary.

It was unfair, really. He knew so much about her but he'd never revealed much more to her than an ex who didn't really like his family and a bizarre fondness for Mr. Collins that she hadn't been able to talk him out of during their hours in the car. The rest of what she knew about him could be counted on one hand, all gleaned from just a few conversations. His parents had adopted him, they died over ten years ago, and he worked at the hardware store—which she'd been avoiding despite three burned out lightbulbs and a leaky sink.

Compared to what he knew about her, it was like he was a stranger.

"Thank you for the plant."

"It's an orchid. In a self-watering pot."

"What? How does that work?"

He explained the principle briefly.

This, for some reason, was what finally brought tears to her eyes. "You could have just mentioned these pots months ago and none of this would have happened."

His eyebrows drew together. "I'm so sorry. You have to know that. I never meant to take away someone you counted on for support."

That last bit didn't quite make sense to her fuzzy, stuffy head. It also didn't make sense why she wished his hands were wrapped around her instead of in tight fists at his side. She made her way to the couch and curled up on it to cry, not caring at this point that he could see her. It still hurt so much and she didn't know if she could talk about it, if she could hear him say the words.

"Why was it so easy?"

She couldn't see him behind her, still standing in the kitchen awkwardly, but she heard him move, the rustle of his clothes as he shifted positions.

"Why what was so easy?"

"Lying to me."

The soft whoosh of his exhale was too far away for her to feel it, yet her skin prickled anyway at the sound.

"It was the hardest thing I've ever done."

"That's hyperbolic."

"Well, it's true." There was an edge to his voice, not unkind, but firm. "It was why I pushed you away that night you kissed me. I hated feeling like I knew so much about you but I was keeping this huge thing from you."

Juliet rubbed her temples. Thinking about that night was the last thing she wanted to do now. She was sick, and tired, and dressed in book pajamas with a plaid coat thrown over them, and her hair hadn't been washed in almost a week. The memory of his lips on hers, his hands around her, was too much.

"There are other things I haven't been able to tell you, which isn't fair when you've shared so much with me. I want to tell you about things that have happened to me, with the account, with my life. They don't excuse anything, but—"

"Just stop." She could tell he was gearing up for some big, emotional moment, getting things off his chest. Revealing things in a dramatic Mr. Darcy kind of way, with the hope of changing her mind about him, about how she felt.

She simply didn't have the energy. "I'm too sick for this."

Lucas shifted on his feet, uncertainty flickering across his face. He opened and closed his mouth a few times before looking down at his feet. "Should I go then?"

"I think that's best."

"Can I come back?"

"I don't know but . . . I don't think so." It was just too hard.

She heard his slow steps toward the door. She heard it open.

"I'm here if you ever need me."

The door closed.

Before she crashed into the couch in a hazy, sniffly mess, she knew the last person she needed right now was Lucas.

TWENTY-FIVE

The room was beige, the chairs were beige, and tables were beige. There wasn't a spec of color anywhere besides the clothes the members of the garden club were wearing.

It was their first meeting in the new space, and the mood of the room seemed to fit Lucas perfectly: tired, sad, blah. No one was happy with the new space, least of all him.

Granny was the only one who seemed cheerful despite their setting. She went through the agenda topics with her usual sunny efficiency, calling on a few different members to present on various topics.

A newer member talked about her experiments with growing houseplants in glass jars using only water. The second longest member showed off her late spring tulips and reminded everyone about the bulb exchange event later in the summer. The treasurer reported what Sage had already told him, that their recent plant sale and community fair table had netted them more than enough to afford this new location for a few years.

Lucas should feel relieved. The club would be fine. They

weren't homeless. But this was the furthest thing from a home you could get.

Any space in his brain not stewing over the garden club's fate was completely occupied with Juliet. The visit with the cookies had been a total failure. It seemed like the perfect plan after what Sage had said. He'd explain how much the breakup with Audrey had messed with his head and how being the oldest in his huge family made him feel like he had to do everything for everyone, especially with his parents gone.

The problem was that she didn't know enough about him, so he'd been ready to bare his soul, tell her whatever she wanted to know. Give her a Darcy-level outpouring of information that would totally change her mind about everything.

But she hadn't even let him speak.

The rejection hit hard, even days later. While garden club meetings usually lifted his mood, today it was just making everything worse.

His head snapped up when he heard his name.

"We have Lucas to thank for this," Granny said.

Everyone was smiling at him and clapping, but he'd completely missed why. His eyes darted to Mari across the room, who merely raised an eyebrow at his confused expression. As promised after his mini meltdown last week, his cousins were all taking a more active part in the club, to relieve a bit of the pressure on him.

"Your work with . . . the Friends made sure we preserved some of the most precious memories of the club. Thank you, my darling boy."

Granny's hesitation over her phrasing was like a kick in the gut. Of course she'd want to say Juliet's name, but assumed Lucas wouldn't want to hear it. But Juliet was the real reason so much had been saved. With her eagle eyes and tender heart, everything that truly mattered had made its way to the boxes in Granny's garage.

Juliet had done everything she could to help both the Friends and the garden club, while Lucas had spent his time working to help only his people. That's all he ever did, he realized. There were the people and causes he cared about, and you were either with him or against him. All the lying about Plantsguy95 had been in service of some personal vendetta Lucas had created for no good reason, and had ended up pushing away someone he really cared about.

From the start, Juliet had confused and frustrated him because she was so squarely in the middle. She liked plants but also books. She was part of this town, but didn't know many people. She was his but she wasn't.

He shifted in his seat, guilt squishing in his gut as everyone looked at him with smiles of appreciation.

What would they all say if they knew what he'd done? None of this would have happened if he just put his face or name on his account. Why was he so afraid of anyone knowing? Because Audrey had mocked him two years ago?

It seemed like a flimsy excuse after the mess he'd made of things. Yes, it had hurt when he hadn't made his account the success she'd wanted, but she would have left him for some other reason eventually, he realized now.

Granny was talking again, and Lucas shifted his attention to her. "Now, we all have our own special memories of Maude, but I brought some of the boxes for everyone to go through together and choose something to take with them."

This was news to Lucas. He stood, not understanding how she'd been able to get the boxes here on her own, and he stood up, his heart beating wildly. Granny waved him down. "It's all taken care of, Lucas dear, don't worry."

It felt like Lucas spent his whole life worrying sometimes. The conversation with his cousins had been playing on a loop in his brain for the last week. They'd offered to help him with the Plantsguy95 account since it was stressing him out so much, but he hadn't even considered that as an option.

The last few years, he'd found joy and satisfaction in connecting with people online, in teaching and learning about plants. It was something outside of his family or the club that didn't help them directly, and he realized now he'd felt guilty about that. Like he wasn't allowed to have something just for himself. Like all his time had to be dedicated to others, or he wasn't enough for them.

Who knew there'd be so many emotions wrapped up in his one little social media account?

There was a knock on the door and Denise stuck her head into the room. "You ready for the boxes?"

Lucas frowned. A glance at Mari told him she was just as confused. Obviously Granny and Denise had been in contact about the house, but now that the cleanup was over, there was no reason for the two groups to be working together.

That's the kind of thinking that got you into this mess.

A line of high schoolers flowed into the room and deposited a stack of ten boxes at Granny's feet at the front of the room.

"Thank you, Denise, thank you, young ladies."

They all filed out of the room and the twenty-or-so garden club members looked expectantly at Granny, who waved them all to the front. "Now don't be shy. Come grab a box and take a look."

While everyone else shuffled out of their seats, Lucas stayed put. The urgency he'd had before when putting things into those boxes was gone. Now every piece held not only memories of Maude, but of Juliet as well and how he'd wasted all that time together. Instead of the petty needling, he could have shared more with her, tried to partner like Granny and Denise.

Throughout the days they'd spent together, she'd been open and willing, while he still kept so much back. And not just the Plantsguy95 thing. He'd barely told her anything about his past, Audrey, his family. He had his small circle of people he trusted, and no one else had been let in since so long he couldn't remember.

What was so scary about telling her those things? She might not like what she heard? Well, too late for that.

With a thump, Mari dropped a box next to him, pulling him out of his thoughts.

"You look miserable. Like you didn't get the last rose and have to go home to the D-level stardom of a former *Bachelorette* contestant."

He rubbed the back of his neck. "Is she back at *Bachelor* nights?" He knew she wouldn't tell him, but he couldn't help asking.

Mari shook her head. "You're not getting that info. The Geis Gals have meddled enough. We've decided never again."

He raised an eyebrow and she chuckled.

"Okay, fine, not never, but we're definitely staying out of this. Here." She nudged the box with her toe. "Some distraction. This one wasn't from the house. It's stuff she left Granny."

"Doesn't she want to keep it all?"

Mari shrugged. "She wanted us to see if there was anything in here the club could use. I think it's mostly papers and journals, so something she wanted the family to look through first."

They each took a stack and started to shift through. There were pictures from garden club events, Maude's travels, and birthdays with the Geis cousins. A grim-faced man Lucas didn't recognize was in a few photos with a very young and unusually smiley Maude. He held one up to show Mari.

"Who's this with Maude? She looks like you when you talk about your boyfriend."

Mari rolled her eyes but also flushed, and his stomach lurched. Teasing his cousin had the opposite intended effect of lifting his mood. He stuck his hand back in the box and pulled out a stack of notebooks. The journals were from the years 1955, 1963, and 2007, which seemed odd. Though if she'd left them to Granny, they must mean something.

Remembering how the house had been organized, however, it could be a random selection of journals. A familiar zing of pain hit his chest thinking about the house and Juliet again.

He groaned and buried his head in his hands. "I really messed up. Tell me how to fix it?"

"Nope." Mari's lips smacked on the word, her nose buried in a journal. Suddenly, she looked up and grabbed his arm. "Lucas, look at this."

She passed him the book, the feathery scrawl a little hard to read. It took him a few minutes to fully take in what was on the page. When he looked up at Mari, her eyes were bright.

"Do you think Granny knew about this?"

"Only one way to know. Let's go ask her."

They made their way through the maze of chairs and people bent over boxes to where their grandmother sat at the front of the room. Excitement buzzed in his chest, the first positive emotion he'd had in days.

It wouldn't solve what to do with Juliet, but this tiny ray of light in the gloom of the last few weeks was enough to put a smile on Lucas's face. Granny returned it when he and Mari approached her.

As the two cousins debated with the doyenne of their family on the next steps, warm hope spread into Lucas's chest. There was still a lot of work to do, discussions to be had, and more long days inside. It would mean working with Denise even more, which Lucas was nervous about since he probably wasn't her favorite person, but it was a possible solution to a lot of problems.

If this could all work out, then there had to be a way for him and Juliet. He just had to keep digging.

TWENTY-SIX

The tension was high, and eight pairs of eyes were focused on Juliet.

"Well, what do you think?"

Juliet shifted on the couch, unsure which of the final bachelorettes she should name as her pick. There was an unusual amount of anxiety thrumming in her veins about what should have been a simple decision. Except it wasn't simple, not when the votes were split evenly and they were all looking to Juliet for the tiebreaker.

"Um, Ashley, I guess?"

"You guess?" Lily shrieked, her twin echoing the sentiment.

Meanwhile, Violet smiled widely. "She's made her choice. The quiet girl wins."

"She hasn't won yet." Lily flopped back on the couch, a slight pout on her face.

Mari leaned in to whisper in Juliet's ear. "She'll get over it. We've predicted the winner the last five seasons."

The anxiety dissipated once Juliet realized this was just part of the Geis traditions she was slowly being wrapped up in. Traditions that had nothing to do with Lucas.

Lily sat up, a hand in the air. "We still need to get Lucas's vote." With a gasp, she turned to Juliet. "Never mind."

It was the first time any of them had mentioned him since Juliet had returned to *Bachelor* nights. Though it was what she'd wanted, and the gatherings contained more gossiping about the show than about their lives, it had felt like they'd been tiptoeing around it anyway. Now that Lily had broken the seal, a rush of other comments followed.

"None of us are talking to him right now."

"Well, except to get him to help us with plants."

"Or picking up something in his truck."

"Or that time last week I forgot my phone at work and he swung by to pick it up."

"Even so, we're all still super mad."

"But mostly really sorry we knew about his terrible plan and didn't tell you sooner."

Juliet couldn't help it. She burst out laughing. It was sweet how much they were trying to be on her side. But they were on his side, too, and didn't even know how not to be.

"It's okay, really. I'm over it. Over him."

Sage and Heather exchanged glances with Mari. "Really?" Heather asked. "Like, over him, over him?"

"Yeah." There was a dip in Juliet's stomach. Would they not want to hang out with her now? "Is that ok?"

"Oh, completely and totally fine." The words rushed out of Sage, the others nodding along. "It means less drama between the garden club and the Friends, so it's a relief really."

"Why would there still be drama?" Now suddenly no one wanted to meet her eyes. "He's not still campaigning for the house, is he?"

"I don't think so." With a quick glance at Mari, Sage continued. "He and Granny have been meeting with Denise a lot, but it could just be about how to take care of Maude's plants. Since you're over him, it doesn't really matter, right?"

Denise hadn't mentioned anything, but there were a lot of other volunteers in the Friends. One of them was probably helping with the plants. Stephen, or his husband even. There was no reason for Juliet to get involved anymore. Especially considering how much she'd embarrassed herself at the community fair with that whole ridiculousness with the signs.

"If he was doing anything to sabotage the Friends, you'd tell me, right?"

"Absolutely."

There was no hesitation in Sage's words. Juliet's shoulders relaxed. "I'm sorry, I don't mean to make you all choose sides."

"There aren't any sides." Mari's eyes flicked to the television, and she grinned. "Well, except in *The Bachelor*."

"This isn't *West Side Story*," Heather said. "People can be friends with whoever they want, loyal to more than one person, one family, one organization, one town, one country. Love isn't a pie with limited slices."

Juliet flushed at the word love. She never used it with friends, but realized she did love these women in a different way than she did, say, the proper use of apostrophes. Or the way she'd thought she'd loved Lucas for about an hour.

"That's what I've been trying to tell Lucas forever." Sage shook her head. "But he'll go all in on something and refuse to let go once it's a part of him."

That's what Juliet had liked most about him, she suddenly realized. With a stabbing in her chest, she remembered how it felt to realize she wasn't one of those things, and how much she wished she had been.

The others nodded. "Congenital stubbornness."

There was no more time for talk as the show came back from commercials, and it left Juliet plenty of time to think. As predicted, Ashley was indeed moving on to the finale, and everyone erupted into cheers, though Lily's were just a weak clap of her hands.

"He brought me cookies last week when I was sick."

The words flew out of Juliet's mouth before she could stop them. Eight heads turned to her.

"He tried to tell me about . . . I don't know, his life, I guess. I didn't let him talk."

There was a long, semi-uncomfortable silence. When no one from the usually very chatty group commented, Juliet's heart started to race and the words kept tumbling out.

"That was probably rude, wasn't it? I mean, he came all that way, with cookies, and a plant—Oh, I forgot to mention the plant, didn't I? Well, he brought a plant, too."

As the group continued to stay silent, the muted television flashing the intro scenes to the show that always came after *The Bachelor*, Juliet relaxed a little. They were doing the one thing she needed, the thing she hadn't been willing to do for Lucas.

Listening.

So she kept talking.

"Anyway, I feel kind of bad now, he didn't get to say whatever he wanted to say. I don't think he'll try again. But now I guess I am kind of wondering what he wanted to tell me? You know, since I'm over him and it wouldn't really make a difference now, I might as well do the polite thing and listen to him, right?"

It was more words in a row Juliet had said in front of a group in a long time. It was liberating, freeing in a different way than sobbing in Charlotte's arms had been. The quiet acceptance of everything inside of her was soothing, and she took a deep breath, calming the last of her shaking nerves.

"It's just, you said he never lets go of something that he cares about, and it feels like he let go of me." Tears appeared in the corners of her eyes, which was ridiculous, since she was absolutely, definitely over him. "I must have blown my chance the other day, messed things up like I always do."

"You didn't mess anything up," Mari said. The warmth in her gaze was even more soothing than the group silence had been. "This was a weird situation from the beginning. It's not like the typical boy meets girl, boy insults girl where she can overhear him, boy proposes in the most insulting way possible and loses girl, kind of situation."

Juliet's lips curled up in a smile. "You read *Pride and Prejudice?*"

"After hearing him complain about how boring it was, then sitting through the movie with him, yes, I decided I had to read it myself." Mari looked around. "All of us did."

"I'd already read it," Violet said from the corner of the room. "Several times."

"Show off," mumbled someone, and there were a few eye rolls and head nods among her cousins.

"The point is," said Sage, using what Juliet had come to recognize as her 'I'm the oldest so listen to me' voice, "while we normally have a lot to say about, well, everything, this was a unique situation in the history of Geis drama."

Instead of feeling relieved, Juliet was forlorn. "So you don't know if Lucas will try again?"

"Do you want him to?" asked Sage. "After all, if you're over him, it shouldn't matter, right?"

"Right." Juliet shook her head. "You're right. Just let him know I didn't mean to be rude. I was really sick when he came over. I just hope I didn't hurt his feelings too much."

Mari smiled gently. "We'll tell him."

When she left a little while later, everyone gave Juliet a hug, which she wasn't expecting. They didn't say anything other than goodbye, but the extra attention warmed her to her very center, patching up some of the cracks that had formed in her heart over the last few weeks.

Juliet wasn't sure what it would take to mend herself completely, but remembering that she still had a few friends in Greenhaven was a good start.

TWENTY-SEVEN

"I look forward to working more closely with you." Lucas shook Denise's hand and made his way out of Maude's house. He'd never be able to think of it as belonging to the Friends, even if it technically did now.

At least he would be seeing more of the house than he'd have ever hoped just a few weeks ago. There were still details to work out, but he'd leave that to Granny.

Like he probably should have from the start.

Feeling light and cheerful, he hopped into his truck and headed to work.

The drive through town took him close enough to Juliet's apartment that he could swing by with just a minute or two of a detour. He resisted, however, knowing just how creepy that would be. Showing up unannounced once was dramatic and possibly romantic. Showing up twice was borderline desperate.

Though the message he'd gotten from Mari had given him a sliver of hope he might still have a chance. All his cousin had told him during their last lunch date was that "Juliet's sorry if she hurt your feelings." Which meant that she cared about his feelings, and that she was still thinking about his visit.

The idea he had for next steps with Juliet had taken some time to figure out, especially since he'd decided to not ask any of his cousins for their advice. Which could mean it was a terrible plan.

Not asking anyone for their input, figuring it all out on his own, was more terrifying than he'd expected. The actual plan itself wouldn't be a walk in the park either.

He turned into the parking lot of the hardware store and let out a long, slow sigh. There was only one thing to do, one way he could think of to show her that the lying had been more about his own insecurities than it had ever been about getting Maude's house back.

No one who knew him would ever accuse him of being shy, but he'd been hiding behind his anonymity online for far too long. The fear of rejection, the fear of upsetting people in town, the fear of someone saying the same things Audrey had said were all looming over him like palm leaves blocking the sun in his backyard.

The fear of losing Juliet forever was stronger, however, which was the only thing that got him out of his truck and into work. His plan had several steps, and the first one involved asking Henry for a big favor. One that would likely mean working until close for the next few weeks, but hopefully it would be worth it.

There were plenty of plants in his backyard, but Lucas had wanted the setting to be absolutely lush. He didn't want there to be any doubt that he was Plantsguy95. Going overboard with the planters and leafy palms was step one. Thanks to Henry, Lucas had been able to borrow enough to turn his yard into a jungle.

Henry, it turned out, was a total softie, especially when

given several dozen of Granny's cookies. As long as Lucas promised to bring the plants back before the store opened—and didn't tell Henry's dad—then he could take as many as he wanted, as often as he wanted.

Lucas set everything up, sat down in front of the leafiest of the ferns he'd brought outside, took a deep breath, and hit record on his phone.

"Hey there, just wanted to pop on to say hi to everyone. I know it's been a strictly plants-only account for a while, so I thought it was time to share the face behind the photosynthesis." Somehow, he kept the smile on his face, despite the horrendous pun. There were more coming, so people had to be prepared.

It took only another minute or two to finish everything he had to say for this first video. Posting it took just a few taps of his fingers, and then it was done. He let out a long, slow breath. For better or worse, his face and name were out there now. Even if Juliet didn't see it, others in town likely would. Word would get around, and whatever happened, happened.

Then it would be time for step two.

Pete the prayer plant was dying again.

Being sick for a week, then a last-minute, urgent request from a repeat client had kept Juliet off her regular schedule. The only break had been *Bachelor* night last week, and only because Mari happened to send a reminder text right when Juliet was taking a break.

She'd put her BOC on the shelf right next to Pete. It was sparkling in the fading afternoon sunlight, whereas Pete was lackluster and drooping. The contrast was a harsh reminder that she couldn't have it all.

The ability to sort and pick out the best of something could only apply to one area of her life at a time. If she hadn't been so focused on work, on winning the award, she might have spotted Lucas's subterfuge earlier.

She had to accept that she could have friends or work or love, but not all three at once. Two seemed to be her max, and love was obviously out of the picture for a while. Friends were good. The Geis Gals were great.

But could any of them help her with Pete?

Asking Mari, or Sage, or someone else in the garden club was an option. Unless they didn't know what to do, and they asked Lucas for his advice. Even if they didn't tell him who the help was for, he'd probably guess. He knew her well enough, though she still felt like there was so much more to him she'd never get to learn.

She didn't want him to know that she'd failed at this. It was like killing Pete yet again was proof that whatever had existed between Juliet and Lucas was truly dead.

Of course she could find someone else on social media. But she wouldn't know if their advice was worthwhile.

In a fit of desperation, she went to his account. Not to send a message, but just . . . to take a look.

She'd had him muted since the night of the awards. It felt gentler than unfollowing. Besides, he'd have noticed that, and she didn't want him to notice her at all. She was over him, just like she'd told his cousins. So there was no reason not to go to his page now, to see if there was some tidbit she could glean that might help Pete.

This was the first time she'd been to his page in a few weeks, and she was surprised to see so many new posts. Even more surprising was that most of them had his face. And they were videos.

Her heart thundered to think of why he would make such a

change. He'd been anonymous for years, and now to suddenly put his face out there . . . Juliet shivered. She could never do something like that.

It was a simple tap to watch the first one. His voice floated into the quiet of her office, a soothing deepness that her heart recognized instantly. Her shoulders relaxed, and she took in this little snippet of him, not realizing just how much she'd missed his words in her life.

There was nothing shocking or surprising about what he said, though his plant puns were truly terrible. A smile slowly lifted her lips, and she watched another video, then another.

They were short, just him talking to the camera about plants, or his work, or the garden club. Some showed parts of Greenhaven where the garden club had installed benches or flowers, and some were how-to videos where he usually ended up knocking over his camera or spilling water or soil all over himself.

He started all of them with, "Hey, it's Lucas, Plantsguy95."

Then she got to a few where there was no talking, just words on the screen in front of images of plants, all set to music. These were more serious, where he shared how he'd started the account to impress his girlfriend but she'd left him anyway, and how losing his parents so young had made him retreat into his inner circle of family and friends, never letting anyone new in. How it had made him protective of that circle, but most of all, of his own heart.

She stood up from where she'd been huddled on the couch, watching without moving for what was now close to an hour.

Was this what he'd been trying to tell her? It was such a public way to share these private parts of his life, the same things she'd been wondering about for weeks. Heat rushed to her face, even though she was alone.

It was ridiculous to think he'd do something like this just for her. He had tens of thousands of followers, and maybe he just felt like it was time to pivot, to try the vulnerable, real-person marketing a lot of influencers used. Soon he'd start selling something, using his back story as the hook to draw people in, make the move from hobby to business.

Then she watched them all again and noticed the music. The first video had a song called "Hey Juliet" visible in tiny script at the top of the screen. Her heart started to pound. It could have been a mistake. The melody was upbeat and went well with his fumbling with the camera and his planters.

When she saw the next video with a song titled "Sorry," she held her breath.

The next few videos all had instrumental music, which Juliet instantly recognized as the soundtrack to *Pride and Prejudice*.

She dropped her phone.

It was all for her.

Retrieving her phone from the couch cushions, she sent the first one to Charlotte, who Juliet knew would be online right now. It felt like an eternity before her phone dinged with a reply.

EDITSALOTTIE

I was wondering when you'd notice these.

JCEDITS

What should I do?

EDITSALOTTIE

What do you want to do?

JCEDITS

I don't know! It can't really be all for me, can it?

EDITSALOTTIE

He lost over 8k followers last week.

He's definitely not doing it for the views.

JCEDITS

Now I feel terrible.

I should have just listened when he came over.

Then he wouldn't have had to tell the whole world about Audrey and his parents.

EDITSALOTTIE

Maybe he needed to do it in a bigger way.

Not just for you, for him.

At least, that's what Charlie said.

JCEDITS

What else does Charlie say?

EDITSALOTTIE

That if I'd ever made fun of him the way it sounds like Lucas's ex did, he'd never show his face online.

Wounded pride is hard to get over. Just ask Charlie and his old football friends.

He thinks this is a way for Lucas to show his ex he doesn't care what she thinks anymore, just as much as it's a way for him to get you a message too.

That made sense, even if Juliet wouldn't have chosen this particular method herself. The scars past relationships left on you looked different for everyone, and healing them looked different too. She'd gotten into a car for the first time in over a year, all thanks to Lucas. Now he was telling the world who he was and taking credit for his account when he'd been told he wasn't good enough, when he felt like he'd have the laser gaze of his whole family and community on him watching for any sign of failure.

All thanks to Juliet.

That kind of courage couldn't go unrecognized. Taking a deep breath, she quickly hit the heart icon on every single one of his videos. He'd have hundreds of notifications from his thousands of followers, but hopefully her name would stand out, to let him know she'd seen him. She'd seen him and she was ready to listen again.

TWENTY-EIGHT

"She's not going to come." Lucas looked at his watch for the fifth time in as many seconds.

"If she doesn't, then she doesn't." Heather shrugged. "Nothing you can do about it."

After countless hours of discussion with Denise, Granny, and Mayor Taylor—who Lucas had to promise to not call again about anything for at least two years—the Periwinkle Mansion was now an extension of the community center. It was still owned by the Friends, and they had the majority of the upstairs rooms for their book storage and programming. The rest of it was available for use by the different groups in the town as needed. The garden club would still get to hold their meetings there, along with other organizations, and new happy memories would fill the house for years to come.

It was what Maude had talked about with George Thomas, the founder of the Friends, back in 1963. Her journals from that year held detailed descriptions of their plans for joint projects, like including some of the club's horticultural drawings in the library's literary magazine. But then he'd died suddenly that summer and she'd never mentioned him again. Not even to Granny.

This had led Lucas and his cousins to speculate George may have been more than a friend to Maude, but they'd never know. All they could know with some certainty was that "for community use" in Maude's will meant that while her gift to the Friends was a way to honor George, she'd probably never intended the house to only be used by the Friends.

So Lucas had presented the larger community center project to everyone involved, worked for weeks to finalize all the details with them, and the grand opening was today.

He'd done everything he could think of to make sure Juliet knew about it. He'd put it all over his posts, told his cousins, and the Friends would obviously know through Denise.

But that didn't mean she'd come.

It had been two weeks since she'd like-bombed his videos, and he knew she still saw all the new ones. He'd been holding back on reaching out though, just in case it didn't mean what he hoped it did.

Since she hadn't done anything other than like his posts, it was much more likely all it meant was that she wasn't totally mad and that if she saw him around town she wouldn't cross to the other side of the street.

Except he hadn't seen her around town, not even at Cork and Beans on Wednesday afternoons, where he'd just happened to be stopping by to pick up some coffee before work. And after work. And during his break.

He stabbed his hands through his hair. Not being mad wasn't the same as wanting to be with him.

"Go get some food, you're making me nervous by pacing back and forth like that." Sage appeared next to him with a plate of cheese and veggies in her hand. When he waved away her offering, she let out a long sigh. "Oh, for the love of ferns, she's coming. She's been busy with work, you big dummy, that's why she hasn't written to you."

"What?" He turned so quickly, he knocked her plate to the floor. The glare he got from Sage was one of her worst.

Without being asked, he hurried to pick everything up and go get her a new one from the kitchen, his pulse racing. She was coming. Why hadn't they told him before? Probably to torture him. Or, perhaps, they really were trying to stay out of his business, as promised.

When he came out from the kitchen with a new plate for Sage, he almost dropped it again. Juliet was standing with his cousins, laughing and chatting with all of them. He overheard the word "final rose" so they must be discussing the finale from a few days ago.

Her terracotta hair glowed fiery red in the sunlight streaming through the large bay windows of the living room. Even from a distance, he could see the way her green eyes sparkled, the happiness that was in them from talking with her friends. His family.

Taking a deep breath, and reminding himself to play it cool no matter if she acknowledged him or not, he stepped into the group and held out the plate.

"Here you go, Sage."

His cousin took the plate but frowned. "You forgot the crackers." When he turned, she held out a hand. "Don't worry. I'll go get them. Heather, can you help me?"

"Help you get crackers?" The youngest Geis cousin blinked a few times. Sage arched an eyebrow. "Oh. Yes, I will go help you, over there, in the other room."

Lucas closed his eyes and remembered he loved his family, even if he didn't always like them.

"There must be a pretty large cracker selection in there."

He opened his eyes to see Juliet looking up at him, a slight upward tilt to her lips.

"Sage is particular about which carbs she combines with cheese."

"Yes, I've noticed that during our *Bachelor* nights."

It was almost like it had been before, the light banter, but not quite. There was a thin wall still up, but Lucas couldn't tell if it was on her side or his. Maybe both.

The silence stretched, the endless unsaid topics swirling in the air around them like pollen in a shaft of sunlight.

"If you're still mad, just say the word and I'll stop," he blurted out. "You can block me, whatever."

Her eyes flicked down, and her bottom lip tucked under her teeth. "Mari told me you didn't tell any of them about what you were going to do. With the videos."

"They probably would have told me not to."

"Would you have listened?"

"Probably not. I needed to do my own thing. Make up my own mind about stuff."

She looked up at him again, eyes wide with a question.

"This is about me, not all of them. And you, if you want it to be."

"And if I don't want it to be?"

His heart sank, but he kept looking at her, not breaking her intense gaze. "One word from you will silence me on this subject forever."

Her gaze narrowed. "Is that a line from *Pride and Prejudice?*"

"Depends. Did it work?"

She took a step toward him and inhaled deeply. Something about the smell of the house—a mix of plants and books Lucas had always loved—must have pleased her, because a wide grin spread across her face.

"I think you're much more like Mr. Collins," she said.

"Excuse me?" He put his hands on his hips and glared down at her.

"Well, you used to be." She giggled, and every tightly coiled muscle in Lucas relaxed. "You cared a lot about what others thought of you."

"I still do."

She raised an eyebrow at that.

"I want to be totally honest with you." He closed the distance between them. "I will be. Forever, if you'll let me."

Holy Hoya, that was cheesier than the plate he'd made Sage, but it seemed to be the right thing to say. She reached up and wrapped her arms around his neck. Sparks of light burst in his chest, and it was only the weight of her hands on his shoulders that kept him from floating away.

"I think that sounds like something I might be interested in."

The room was empty, but there was no guarantee it would be for long. Taking his chance, Lucas leaned down, brushing his mouth against hers, intending only for it to be a brief peck, a promise of something more, of countless other kisses to come.

The second their lips touched, however, that same electricity from when she'd kissed him rippled through his body. Her arms tightened around his neck, and this time, he wrapped her snugly in his embrace like he'd wanted to all those weeks ago.

She knew him and she still wanted him. There was no better feeling than that.

Though the kiss was a very close second.

The scrape of a chair from another room finally pulled them out of what was quickly turning into a very inappropriate display for a community event. And the mayor had only just forgiven Lucas for the sign incident.

He kept his arms wrapped around her though, even as a few people wandered into the room, cups and plates in hand.

He smiled down at her. "So you talked to my cousins about me?"

"We live in a pretty small town, Lucas. The only thing to do here is visit each other and gossip about people." Her eyes glittered with humor. "Should we give them something good to talk about?"

She leaned in to kiss him again, and the world melted away. He'd hear about it from his cousins, Granny, the mayor. But all of that didn't matter. What mattered was what he wanted for himself, and by some miracle of technology, he'd found it in Juliet.

And he was never letting go.

EPILOGUE

"Hi, Juliet," Patrice said, and waved from where he was bundled up in a rocking chair on the porch, a blanket over his lap.

She stumbled on the steps up to the Periwinkle Mansion. The only reason she didn't fall was because Lucas was holding her hand.

"You okay?" His voice was low and rumbly in her ear.

She nodded, still feeling a little unsteady, and waved back at Patrice. Being recognized by people around town shouldn't please her so much, but it still did. She might never get used to it.

Lucas let go of her hand to put his arm around her shoulder and gave her a squeeze.

She definitely wasn't used to *that* yet, even all these months later.

They were on their way to the first planning meeting of a joint book and plant sale. The event in the spring had been so successful for both organizations that Denise and Mrs. Geis had thought about doing it on purpose this time.

When she walked into the room, Juliet felt at home in a way she'd never imagined she could feel. Even in her hometown growing up, there'd been that feeling of being on the outside, growing up in the shadow of a bright older sister.

In Greenhaven, Juliet could be her odd little self, and had found people just like her. Well, not exactly like her, but odd in their own endearing ways.

The meeting was short, but they lingered long after, talking to Stephen and his husband, the Geis cousins, and others from both groups who were all pleased about the joint effort.

Back outside in the brisk January afternoon, Lucas pulled her into a kiss, where the familiar warmth spread through her limbs and turned them to jelly. It was all she could do to stay upright, and she clung to his muscled arms as her knees wobbled. Breaking the kiss, he held his phone high and snapped a quick picture of her looking up at him all gooey-eyed.

"Don't you *dare* post that." She jumped for the phone, but he held it high, out of her reach.

"Of course not. This is for my own personal collection. So I have something to remind me of you when you disappear for days to work."

She'd gotten better about taking breaks, so those long sprints were rarer now, but he never complained when they happened. He would simply show up at her apartment to water her plants and to feed her, if her mother hadn't already.

"And what do I have to remind me of you while you're at the store?"

"You have Plantsguy95," he said, smirking. After an initial dip in followers, his account was bigger than ever, thanks to the magical combination of plants and his tendency to wear short-sleeved shirts that showed off his tattoos and muscles as he explained why good drainage was so important.

It was him, but it wasn't all of him. Juliet was the only one who got to see that.

"I prefer Lucas, though."

"Really?" Even now, there was still a hint of disbelief in his voice. Maybe he still wasn't used to having Juliet's love, either.

Not wanting to leave anything unsaid between them, she leaned up to brush her cold nose against his. "Really. I love you."

"I love you too."

Hand in hand, they walked back together through town, toward home.

AUTHOR'S NOTE

Whenever I read a romance novel, I always wonder what's real and what's not.

Yes, I realize the entire point of fiction is that it's made up. But there are always hints of real places, people, and events tucked in between the imaginary dialogue uttered by inexplicably buff and beautiful characters.

In case anyone is as weirdly curious as I am, here's a very short and incomplete list of what's real and not real in this book:

- BOC awards: not real. If they were real, I would definitely nominate my editor Elle, who, among other things, pointed out that professional editors usually nice down and Juliet probably wouldn't have been editing such a wide range at this point in her career. I ignored that, because Elle is a very good editor who always reminds me that it's my book and I can do what I want with it. But freelance copyeditors are a very real thing, and are adored by all writers who know what's good for them (even if we ignore them sometimes).

- Fear of driving in cars: amaxophobia is real, but not what Juliet was dealing with. It was more like how you avoid going to the restaurant where your high school boyfriend dumped you a week before prom (not real...at least, not the restaurant part). For Juliet, the restaurant is being in cars.

- Friends of the Library: very much real! Your town, or a town nearby, probably has one. They more than likely have book sales where you can get cheap used books AND support the library! They probably do other cool stuff too for your library. You should do some Googling and find out.

- Greenhaven: not real, but based on lots of towns I've lived in and visited.

- Garden club plant sales: very real! I bet your town also has one of these. I also bet if they happen the same day as book sales, you can overhear people complaining about it, which is what inspired this book.

- People having mostly online friends they've never met in person: real, at least for me and all my (online, obviously) writer friends. I love all of them and can't even remember at this point who read parts of this book and who simply cheered me on when I was feeling hopeless about it, so here's a giant YOU'RE THE BEST to every single person in my DMs right now.

- #Solvemyplantproblems: not real, unfortunately, and I very much need it. If you start it, please let me know and I will send you pictures of all my dying houseplants.

- *The Bachelor*: real. Confession: I have never watched a single episode, but I love watching people obsess over it on social media. The Geis gals are my love letter to people who unashamedly love reality TV, because it's a thing I wish I could do.

Keep reading for a sample of The Bridesmaid and The Reality Show, *the first book in the* Wedding Games *series that I co-wrote with my writing bestie (who I met online, of course) Kayla Tirrell.*

10 days.
   3 bridesmaids.
   1 dream wedding.
   What could possibly go wrong?

When Audrey Hudson decides to get married on a reality show, her siblings and best friend were ready for drama—but they never expected to find their own love stories along the way.

Chapter 1

10 Days Until Dream Wedding

Sienna was late.

Her t-shirt was inside out.

And she had to pee.

This whole crazy trip was not off to a good start.

She still couldn't believe her sister had agreed to be a partici-pant for the show, *Wedding Games*. Or that it was filming near their hometown.

Sure, the idea of spending ten days in a gorgeous mountain inn with all expenses paid was tempting. And knowing it would all end in an over-the-top wedding that was guaranteed to be the topic of Thanksgiving dinners for years to come also sounded amazing.

But couldn't Audrey see for every reason to agree to be a participant for the show, there were a million other reasons to say no?

This was reality TV, after all. People weren't looking for a smooth, problem-free event. That was too boring—too easy. Viewers wanted drama. They wanted meltdowns.

And the producers of the show were going to make sure their audience got what they wanted by any means necessary. At least, that was the argument Sienna had made when Audrey first called her with the news—an argument she'd voiced even louder once she'd seen the contract she was required to sign.

A film-crew would be allowed all access to the wedding preparations, and everyone in the wedding party needed to sign it if they wanted to be invited to the intimate ceremony. It was frustrating to be forced into a reality TV show, but Audrey was Sienna's sister, for goodness sake. She would't dream of missing her wedding, so she signed the stupid thing, even though it was filled with so much legal jargon, it made her head spin.

Everyone knew drama was what made people keep watching those shows. Viewers hoped the bride would go full-blown crazy. Or that one of the bridesmaids would get jealous of the way everyone fussed over the bride. It was a perfect storm, and Audrey couldn't see it.

But why would she listen to her little sister? It's not like Sienna had first hand experience in the entertainment business—oh wait, yes she did. Sure, it was only a few years, and mostly stage and commercial work, but she knew the industry better than the rest of her family. Maybe Audrey was too blinded by the idea of her happily ever after with Eli, that she didn't consider how difficult this might be for everyone else involved. Sienna had never been in love like that, but had heard it made you do all sorts of crazy things.

Regardless, Sienna loved her oldest sister and was going to support her. She'd packed her suitcase, booked a last-minute red-eye flight from New Jersey to Asheville, and had just finished driving an hour to get to the secluded inn the producers chose for the filming site.

Growing up in the area she'd never even known it was tucked away in the mountains. But someone from up north had bought it last year and it was all her family could talk about. As the destination came into view, Sienna thought it looked more like a mansion that wanted to pretend it was something cozier.

It was a two-story building, with large windows on every side that were sure to give the place the perfect amount of natural light anytime of day. One side of the inn had an impressive stone chimney that took up the entire wall. And way in the distance, Sienna could just see the corner of what looked to be an old barn, set against the backdrop of acres and acres of gorgeous trees and mountains.

With the sun still rising in the distance, the scene was magnificent.

Sienna drove up the gravel path and crossed her fingers that the rental car she'd gotten had enough power to make it up the steep incline to the front of the building. The bumpy road was not helping her bladder situation, which had reached critical levels about ten minutes ago.

She was the last to show up—as usual—and saw a small crowd that consisted of the wedding party gathered out front. The camera crew was still off to the side and mercifully hadn't begun filming yet, as far as she could tell. That meant she had time to take care of her pressing business.

She parked her car beside her mother's familiar and practical beige sedan.

With a deep sigh, and a mumbled, "You can do this," under her breath, Sienna looked in the rearview mirror. She plastered a fake smile on her face and stepped out of her vehicle.

Her mother came rushing over immediately, a look of panic across her face. "Oh, Sienna, there you are," she shrieked. "We've all been wondering if you would ever show up."

"And hello to you too, Mother," Sienna answered, the smile still affixed to her face. "Glad to see you made it here safe."

Her mother huffed as she planted both of her hands on her hips. "Where have you been? It's nearly nine."

A jolt of panic shot through her. "Isn't that what time the contract said to be here?" She could have gotten an earlier flight but it would have made her miss two shifts at work and cost her $200 more. $200 she most certainly did not have.

Her mother shook her head and let out another loud puff of air. "Well, just because they say nine, it doesn't mean that you have to cut it so close." She leaned in and lowered her voice. "You and I both know how much is at stake."

"I know."

The contract was so full of ways things could go badly, it was hard for Sienna to know what exactly her mother was referring to. The right to defamation, the hold clause, the lack of privacy for them but confidentiality for the show. It was all to keep the power in the hands of the producers.

But failing to show up, well, that would potentially pull the plug on the whole thing. Sienna might be notorious for being late, but she wasn't going to risk putting her sister's wedding in jeopardy. Sienna had been so concerned with making it on time, she'd packed everything in a carry-on bag to avoid getting stuck at baggage claim, and hadn't even stopped in the airport bathroom to pee before racing out the doors toward the rental car kiosks. The pressure on her bladder was downright unbearable at this point and she had one mission: Find the little girls room —STAT.

"Well, then let's go." Her mother put her hand on Sienna's shoulder and started to lead her to the rest of the group.

"Actually." Sienna pulled her phone from her back pocket. "I still have fifteen minutes, which means I have just enough time to go to the bathroom."

She pushed past her mother who was mumbling about her disorganized daughters and walked up to the front door of the inn. Nearby, everyone talked excitedly. In her rush, Sienna barely gave anyone more than a passing glance. She did, however, catch Audrey's raised eyebrows and subtle tap of her watch.

Sienna would have plenty of time to catch up, but for right now, she had one thing on her mind. It was like her body sensed a bathroom was close, and had given up all hope of holding it in. If she didn't get to the toilet soon, she was going to give the camera crew a great opening shot.

It was exactly the kind of thing that would happen to her, and she doubted she'd be able to convince the producer not to air something that would provide so much comedy to the high-drama show. Not to mention it was just the kind of thing a casting director might hold against her in a future audition.

No one would hire her as a leading lady in a serious role if ten million viewers had watched her wet her pants. The only thing to do after that would be—shudder—more reality TV. Sienna groaned at the thought as she picked up the pace with a renewed fervor.

After the receptionist at the front desk pointed to where the bathroom was, Sienna practically sprinted down the hall.

Man, I really shouldn't have had so much coffee on the plane.

When she rounded the corner, she bumped into a man, but she couldn't stop to apologize. She needed to pee right this second. He started to say something to her, but she couldn't stop to listen, not with her destination in sight. Sienna whipped the door open and locked herself in the bathroom, relieved to . . . well, relieve herself.

A moan escaped her mouth just as light knock came at the door.

"Wait just a hot second!" she called.

A deep, male voice carried through the door. "I was just going to say—"

"Occupied!"

"—that it's out of toilet paper."

Sienna's eyes snapped to the toilet paper dispenser, and her heart sank as she saw that the man on the other side of the door was right. And of course the bathroom was one of those eco-friendly ones that used air-dryers instead of having a paper towel dispenser.

She sighed. Not only was she going to have to come up with some creative solutions, now, there was someone else who was going to be privy to it. In her rush, she hadn't noticed much about the person, but he sounded like a cranky old man.

She sent up a silent prayer. *Please don't let them be part of the* Wedding Games *crew.*

That would be a sure-fire way to put a target on her head for the entire week.

After figuring out the not-so-convenient logistics of cleaning up without toilet paper, Sienna washed her hands and wiped them on her jeans, too impatient to wait for the weak trickle of hot air to dry them. She ran her fingers through her blonde hair and gave herself a quick once-over before she left the small bathroom. Tilting her head to the side, she pulled her compact out of her purse. It wasn't clear if there would be makeup artists. Reality show or not, there was no way she could be filmed with those bags under her eyes.

Another knock interrupted her concealer application. "Are you okay? Didn't fall in or anything, did you?"

What was this guy's problem?

She put her makeup back in her purse, and opened the bathroom door, ready to give him a piece of her mind. But when she stepped into the hall, she pulled up short. The cranky old man was, in fact, a gorgeous young man. His dark hair barely brushed the tops of the light, blue eyes that were looking directly at her. He was dressed in a simple plaid shirt and jeans that gave away his position as property maintenance—possibly a handyman.

He grinned as he pushed himself off the wall and held out two rolls of toilet paper. "I thought you might need these."

It was too bad those ridiculously good looks didn't come with any sense. It was common courtesy not to interrupt someone while they were going to the bathroom—or wait outside until they were done.

Sienna looked down at the two rolls with a sneer. "And

what? You thought you were just going to bring them in while I was going to the bathroom?"

The guy's smile evaporated. "Sorry for trying to be helpful. I hoped to get them to you in time."

Sienna rolled her eyes. "Well, you did a terrible job."

"I did the best I could considering you ran past me and ignored me as I tried to explain."

"And then you thought it would be a good idea to hang out on the other side of the door? You do know that's, like, creep level ten, right?"

Hurt flashed across his face for the briefest moment before he shook his head. "You know what? I'm not going to stand here and be berated for wanting to help."

With one last pointed look in her direction, the guy stormed off. Sienna stayed glued in her spot and gave him a head start. With any luck, she wouldn't see him again. She'd simply avoid the places where custodians usually hung out, and hope he didn't blab about the rude girl to the rest of the staff. She crossed her fingers she wouldn't find any surprises in her clean sheets tonight.

After waiting in the hall for what she felt was an appropriate amount of time, Sienna joined everyone outside. She ignored the questioning look her mother gave her as she walked over to where Audrey and their middle sister, Harper, were chatting.

Humor danced in Audrey's deep, brown eyes. "You drank too much coffee, didn't you?"

Sienna smiled back at her sister. She knew her addictions well. "Obviously."

"Well, I'm just glad you're here," Audrey said with a quick hug. "I know you weren't too happy about the contract."

"Of course, I'm here." At least *all* her comments over the

past few weeks hadn't been totally ignored. "I wouldn't miss your wedding for anything."

"Mother was about to have a coronary," Harper added. "I swear she checked the time every minute until you got here. I was afraid she was going to call the police to start a search party for you."

Sienna snorted. "It's a wedding. It's not like it's a hair appointment. Even I know how important..."

Her words died off as she spotted a familiar face in the crowd. True, there were a lot of familiar faces here. The group consisted of family and close friends, along with the production crew. There were her sisters and Audrey's best friend Reagan.Reagan's fiancé Harry was talking on his phone, off to the side.

But this face was familiar because Sienna had seen it outside the bathroom only moments earlier.

"Audrey, what's the custodian doing next to Eli?" she asked.

Audrey craned her neck to look around at Eli's parents. "What are you talking about?"

Sienna let out an impatient huff. "The guy with the dark hair who is literally standing next to Eli. Plaid shirt, blue eyes. Why is he out here?"

"Uh, Sienna." Audrey furrowed her brow. "The only person I see over there is Fox. He's Eli's best friend from college."

Eli's best friend? No, that couldn't be right. Even though Sienna lived in New Jersey, she'd met Eli plenty of times. Plus, she followed him on social media like a good future sister-in-law, and not once had she ever seen this Fox guy. She'd remember someone like that. Those eyes weren't exactly something you forget.

Her heart quickened beneath her ribs. "Are you sure?" Sienna asked, her eyes still trained on the guy she'd just argued with as he stood next to Eli.

The two men both wore easy smiles as they talked.

"Are you seriously asking me if I know who my husband-to-be's best man is?"

Best man? Sienna's stomach plummeted. This was so not good.

"Why are you so concerned about the"—Harper lifted her hands and made air quotes—"custodian anyway?"

Sienna felt her cheeks warm. "He was standing outside the bathroom with toilet paper and I thought he worked here." She cleared her throat and added quietly, "I may have been rude to him."

Audrey frowned at her. "Oh, Sienna, you didn't."

She explained what had happened inside, only realizing how quick she'd been to make judgements and serve out punishments once she said it all out loud. A pang of remorse ran through her. She'd acted like a jerk.

Audrey's face was stern, but Harper laughed and waggled her brows. "Looks like the producers won't have to work too hard to get must-see TV from you."

"Shut up." Sienna pushed sister. "I'm sure I can make it through ten days. This is Audrey's special moment."

She needed to remain in control of her emotions whenever a camera was in view. This was her chance to get noticed, but given the expectations of reality shows, it had to be for all the right reasons. There'd be chances to sing and dance, and opportunities to show off her emotional range. One hint of drama and she could kiss any chance at a real career goodbye.

And time was running out on a real career. Sienna and her roommate were skating on thin ice—one more late rent payment and goodbye New Jersey. This reality show was the last thing Sienna wanted to do, but was her only chance to hold onto her dreams.

She could make it through ten days without any drama, right?

Want to keep reading? The entire *Wedding Games* series is out now!

Wedding Games Series (Contemporary Romance):

The Bridesmaid and the Reality Show

The Bridesmaid and the Ex

The Bridesmaid and Her Surprise Love

Free Wedding Games Prequel Novella:

The Wedding Planner's Second Chance At Love

Young Adult Romance:

Rebound Boyfriend

Leah's Song

This Summer at the Lake

Love Lessons

Carnival Wishes

Home for Christmas

ABOUT THE AUTHOR

Daphne James Huff has been writing romance for adult and YA audiences since she was a young adult herself. Her favorite kind of story has a main character who thinks they've got it all figured out until someone barges into their life and messes everything up (Translation: Give her all the enemies-to-lovers books, please!).

Daphne works in HR during the day and fills her nights with reading, baking, and practicing whichever sport she's fallen in love with most recently (2022 was her year of inline skating).

When she's not writing, she enjoys partaking in her hobbies with her husband, son, and cat (though finding skates that will fit the cat has been a bit difficult).

(There are not this many parentheses in her books . . . usually.)

Follow her on Instagram **@daphnejameshuff**

www.ingramcontent.com/pod-product-compliance
Lightning Source LLC
Chambersburg PA
CBHW021148310726
48971CB00002B/536